The Girl
Who Could
Silence
the Wind

The Girl
Who Could
Silence
the Wind

MEG MEDINA

CANDLEWICK PRESS

First paperback edition 2013

Library of Congress Catalog Card Number 2011046080
ISBN 978-0-7636-4602-8 (hardcover)
ISBN 978-0-7636-6419-0 (paperback)

17 18 19 20 21 22 BVG 10 9 8 7 6 5 4 3 2

Printed in Berryville, VA, U.S.A.

This book was typeset in Filosofia.

Candlewick Press
99 Dover Street
Somerville, Massachusetts 02144

visit us at www.candlewick.com

For my mother, Lidia

Contents

Prologue

The curse on Sonia Ocampo's life came without warning before she was even born, cleverly disguised as good luck.

It blew in on one of the worst storms anyone in Tres Montes had ever known. The wind moaned as it bent pine trees in half and stripped them down to bare sticks. Bawling cows were dragged down the mountain on waves of mud, and far below in the canyon, the river swelled and churned like an ocean. The villagers huddled in their swaying houses and cried out their final prayers to any god who might still have pity—all but the Ocampos, who were too busy coaxing a baby into the world.

The tempest—like the birth—raged on for hours. But when at last Sonia Ocampo slipped into the world, blue and shivering, the wind miraculously ceased and the river calmed, leaving behind a peaceful and starry night.

The next morning, the people of Tres Montes were shocked to find themselves still alive. They donned rubber boots and climbed over rubble to reach their church ruins. Each family was counted; not a single life had been lost. No one could explain their survival.

But then they learned of the girl who had arrived in the night.

The elders gathered to inspect the child closely. Wrapped in her grandmother's shawl, she wore the unmistakable look of a sleeping angel.

"She must have been sent to us by God," the old miners proclaimed, unaccustomed as they were to good fortune of any kind, "to protect us from harm."

The coppersmith was ordered to his forge, where he pounded a nugget of metal against his anvil until it revealed the shape of a girl with arms open to world. This was the first milagro ever pinned to Sonia Ocampo. And it was with that simple prick of a prayer charm through her swaddling cloth that her terrible destiny was fixed to her for good.

CHAPTER 1
The Missing Boy

THE TRAIN WHISTLE did not sound through the valley the day Ernesto Fermín's men found Luis. In fact, that morning the whole mountain was unusually quiet. The winter winds had blown in during the night and coated everything in yellow dust. Ghostly buzzards circled for prey over the canyon.

In those days, the train's weekly arrival was still a spectacle for the people of Tres Montes. It crossed the bridge before dawn on Saturday, belching white steam and blowing its whistle to frighten any goats grazing up ahead. Soon after, it would pull into the station, Marco, the handsome conductor, waving like a cinema star over the heads of the bike-taxi boys he'd known all his life. Passengers from far away stepped out to buy pastries and share news from the capital. To Sonia Ocampo, the train meant more than customers for her family's pastries and vegetables. It meant a glimpse at a world she thought she would never know.

She'd been running late that awful morning. Her eyes were heavy for sleep as she crossed the highway and hurried along the winding street. The vigil over a miner's sickbed had lasted all night, much longer than she had expected, but she hadn't had the heart to leave Old Guacho afraid and alone. Even now, as she ran along, she could hear his pitiful groans mixed with the yelps of stray dogs following at her heels. It was as if suffering itself were chasing her.

The rest of her family was already at the plaza, getting ready for market. She spotted her brother Rafael's truck parked against their stall as she arrived. Like everything else, it was coated in dust. Even her brother looked like a spirit.

"Did I miss the train?" she asked him.

He handed down a basket of dusty tomatoes and glanced at the empty tracks through the haze.

"Why do you care?" he replied. "Are you going to moon over Marco like the other girls?" He waved pompously over his head like the conductor.

Sonia pinched his leg. "You're jealous." She squinted to see the farthest point of the tracks and frowned. "It's strange, that's all. Marco never forgets to blow the whistle."

"And who needs *that* racket?" Felix Ocampo said, interrupting them.

Sonia and Rafael exchanged knowing glances as their father joined them at work. Nearly deaf from a lifetime of blasting through silver mines, Felix hated having the cottony peace inside his ears shattered—especially by the train that lured young men to the cities. "A cursed engine of evil" is what he called it. Sonia had long decided that it was pointless to argue with him. Rafael was a different story.

"We do," he grumbled. "It's progress."

"What did he say?" Felix put his ear close to Sonia.

"Nothing, Papi." She shot Rafael a warning look.

But Rafael raised his voice so his father could hear every syllable. "I said, 'It's progress.' The future is out there at the end of the tracks, Papi. Here we're turning to useless dust. See?" He blew a puff of grit from his fender.

Felix glared. "Yes, yes, the *future*," he huffed. "What kind of future is it when boys leave their own families for places unknown? It's a disgrace!" He jutted his chin at Lopez, the milkman, who was hanging cheeses by himself. "Tell me, what father should be left with his hands in his pockets and lonely for his own son?"

Rafael rolled his eyes in plain sight. It would be another quarrel that would change exactly nothing.

"Wipe the sleep from those insolent eyes," Felix snapped. "And watch your mother's *buñuelos*! The woman spent an hour frying them!"

Sonia rescued the tray of her mother's pastries from Rafael's boots as their father stormed off. Two had already been flattened—a stroke of good luck, in her view. She handed Rafael one and took a bite of the other. It was their favorite breakfast.

"Here," she told him. "This might be a sweeter start to the day."

Rafael tore off a piece. "He's wrong."

"He's Papi," she replied before a yawn overtook her. "Sorry."

Rafael studied her tired face as he chewed.

"So, how's Old Guacho?" he asked finally. "You were gone all night again."

Sonia shrugged, wiping jelly from her lips. "The same."

Guacho had mined his whole life like their father. Now his coughs rattled in his chest, and he barely opened his milky eyes. Sonia didn't like to share any of that. Why burden Rafael with dreary reports of dying miners? It would make them both feel strangely old and hopeless. It was better to see her brother laugh, to career down the mountainside on his bike handlebars or hop river rocks when the water wasn't rushing too hard.

"Tell me something," she said, changing the subject. "I notice you look awfully tired yourself. Were you out late again? Doing something I should know about?"

Rafael grinned as he considered his favorite topic. "A little of this and a little of that."

"Oh." Sonia licked her fingers of the last morsels. "A little of *that*. What's her name? Or have you lost track again?"

"Don't worry, *hermanita*." He wiggled his eyebrows. "I have my ways of remembering my girlfriends."

Now it was Sonia who rolled her eyes. "Louse." His last fling—a girl named Dora—had cried over him for a week.

Rafael gave her a quick kiss on the cheek and brushed the dust from her eyelashes. He was a rascal but a charming one.

"Why don't you go home and get some sleep before Mami and Papi find something for you do to?" he told her. "I'll unload the rest."

She shook her head. "Thanks, but no. I think I'll wait for the engine of evil."

Rafael flashed a conspiring grin as he slipped the tray of *buñuelos* on his shoulders. "Suit yourself."

Soon he was moving through the crowd like a waiter in a fine hotel. He looked nothing like a miner, Sonia thought. Not like his father or grandfather or any other Ocampo man before that. It was as if he'd been born into the wrong life entirely.

"¿Buñuelo, guapas?" he called to a few girls, enticing them with his smile and the scent of anise.

A twinge of envy bit at her ribs as he disappeared around the corner. What would it be like to be as carefree as Rafael, to worry about nothing more important than whom to kiss next? Sadly, she would probably never know. She was already sixteen and had never so much as held hands with a boy—all thanks to her destiny.

Sonia pulled her shawl closer and closed her tired eyes, trying not to feel too sorry for herself. The shawl felt like a heavy armor on her shoulders and made her ache for her bed. Hundreds of metal charms were pinned to the threadbare cloth with scarcely the space of a fingernail between them. Mouths to cure a gossip. A heart to find true love. Feet to ensure a safe journey. A fist for strength. So many petitions had been made of her over the years that Sonia had lost count.

She dozed in the gritty breeze, trying to imagine even a simple walk without this weight, but of course that was like imagining a walk without her skin. She'd worn this shawl from the first moment she'd opened her eyes, and today she roamed like a living altar in the mountains. Every step she took jangled with the wishes and hopes of the people who feared what the world had in store for humble ones like them. She was their best hope.

"Bring us back safely, Sonia!" the miners called to her from their trucks each morning.

"This union will bear many healthy children, thanks to you," happy parents cried as Sonia trailed down the aisle behind brides on their wedding day.

"Walk him to the arms of God," Old Guacho's wife had said only yesterday.

"Sonia!"

The voice jarred her awake and nearly toppled her from the flatbed where she'd drifted to sleep.

"Señora Clara?" Sonia said, when she turned and saw who it was.

The woman was wrapped tightly in her own shawl, only her eyes showing. She pressed a charm into Sonia's hand and kissed her fingers reverently.

Sonia looked twice. Gold: a bright yellow piece in the crude shape of a boy. The metal, she noticed, was still warm to the touch.

Dread crawled up her spine as she took in Señora Clara's anguished expression. There was only one way someone so poor could get metal like this. The widow would have a new bloody space in the back of her mouth, a gold-filled molar or bicuspid now missing . . . something not too troublesome to chew without.

Sonia climbed down from the truck, wincing. The sun had heated her charms into branding irons. She pulled the widow into the shade. "What's wrong?"

"He's vanished—like *that*." Señora Clara snapped her trembling fingers. By now the rest of the Ocampos had gathered with the other merchants to listen. Felix sat in a folding chair with his arms crossed proudly; his wife, Blanca, was at his side. Tía Neli sat on an overturned crate and filed her nails as she listened.

"I've asked everywhere, but there is no trace of Luis," Señora Clara continued. "It's been five days since I've seen him."

"Well, is he out chasing skirts?" Tía Neli arched her penciled brow knowingly. "That wouldn't be a first around here."

Blanca Ocampo blushed and poured more tea for Señora Clara. "*Por Dios*, Neli . . . such an idea."

"What?" Tía Neli retorted. "Luis is a young man like any other! Ask Rafael if you don't believe me! He'd know better than anyone." Across the stall, Rafael pretended to stack more peppers, but even from here, Sonia could see his ears were red.

"Let the woman talk, Sister," Felix ordered. He and Tía Neli shared the same dark eyes and sharp tongues, but in everything else they were utter opposites. Not even their mother, Abuela, who visited from the grave in dreams from time to time, had a good explanation for the dueling twins she had left behind. "Five fingers from a single hand, no two the same."

Señora Clara's chin quivered as she spoke of Luis. Her only son had been born with a lame leg, the right foot limp as a dead fish. Of all the young miners, only Rafael didn't mind climbing down the shafts with him—or, on occasion, inside a willing girl's bedroom window.

"If only such a thing were true," she told Tía Neli. "But I've made every hussy in this town swear on the souls of her dead. None has seen him. I . . . I don't know where he could be."

Sonia blinked. From the corner of her eye, she could see Rafael grow still, his jaw clenched.

But you do know, she thought. *We all know.* But as usual, no one had the valor to make a mother face the truth.

Like every boy in Tres Montes, Luis nursed secret fantasies of a life outside the mines. That's what young men talked about—besides girls—as they rode along the serpentine path to the mines. Each year a few lucky ones got working papers for jobs far away, out in the open air—golden boys who sent money back home. But for most, there were no papers. If hunger and imagination nudged them enough, they left quietly on their own to find their way to the capital and beyond, risking robbers who stalked travelers in the valley.

"What do you think is beyond that mountain?" Sonia had asked Luis as they picnicked on the cliffs once. She could still see the last plume of smoke as they'd watched the train disappear for the capital.

"The whole exciting world," he had replied, already enchanted. "What else?"

But how would Luis make a trek through the valley? Steep hills always made him topple despite his special shoe; climbing left him wheezing. Without Rafael as a companion, who would carry his pack? Who would help him over the boulders the way she sometimes did?

"Help me, Sonia." Luis's deep voice suddenly became Señora Clara's, who now knelt at Sonia's feet. She looked so small and pitiful. Her eyes were gentle but frightened in a way that made Sonia's chest ache.

"Please, Señora Clara," she whispered. "Stand up." It always filled her with shame when elders begged her for help.

But Señora Clara only bowed her head lower.

"You'll pray to bring him back to me?"

Every neighbor turned. Alicia, whose husband had finally become faithful. Georgina, whose skin had been cured of oozing sores with Sonia's herbs and prayer. Even Luz, saved from the clutches of a fever in her crib.

"Save my boy's life," Señora Clara whispered. "You are my only hope."

Sonia's mouth went dry. The bones of her shoulders bowed lower still as she reached for the widow's hand. Señora Clara's fingers were long and thin like her son's, but her hands were as icy as those of a corpse.

Felix sprang to his feet. His voice boomed. "Of course she will save him! Take that worry off your heart, *señora*. Sonia has God's ear."

For the rest of the morning, Sonia prayed at the church ruins, where a circle of stones beneath the prickly weeds still marked the spot where she had lain as a newborn. Of all the things she had ever asked for, Luis's safety seemed the most urgent. Guacho, dying in his bed, was an old man. His whiskers had grown white with time; he'd lived out his days longer than most miners. But Luis was young; he was at the beginning of his days.

So as proof of Luis's goodness, she carefully listed for

God every kindness he had shown. She begged pity for his worried mother. She asked for good strangers to help him find his way.

When she was through, she walked wearily back to Rafael, sitting in his truck. He took a long drag of his cigarette and glanced around the market. Then he took her shawl and balled it like a rag in a corner.

"Lie down, Sonia," he whispered. "You need sleep."

She lay back, staring for a long while at the spotless sky overhead. Finally, she turned to him. "Where is Luis?" she whispered. "He left to find work, didn't he?"

Rafael would not meet her gaze. Instead, he tossed away his cigarette butt and crept to her side.

"Sleep." Stretched out alongside her, he hummed the tune Blanca used as their lullaby. It was an old miners' song, one to lift men's spirits over the endless blackness of their days.

It was useless this time. As the afternoon wore on, the air grew hotter, and thick dust swirled in intolerable eddies. The cows would not give a drop of milk. And even the wild parrots that usually roosted happily in the bushes pecked at one another so viciously that Rafael finally shot a pistol in the air to send them off.

But what Sonia noticed most of all was that the train did not arrive.

16

Across the market, Tía Neli put down her magazine. Sonia watched as her aunt marched to the police station at the end of the plaza and rapped loudly on the shutters.

"And when do you plan to do something, Ernesto Fermín?" she demanded at the window. "Being the police captain is more than showing off your medals and that silly gun, you know!"

Capitán Fermín sighed. "What exactly do you expect me to do, Neli?"

"First of all, let me in."

Sonia rolled over as her aunt stepped inside.

Shortly afterward, four of the department's best men set out on horseback, kicking up clouds as they thundered off.

It wasn't long after that.

Sonia was sipping her mother's chamomile tea when Capitán Fermín arrived with the news. He climbed up to the auction platform and removed his worn hat. Beside him stood Marco. The conductor's tie was loose, and his eyes were rimmed in red.

"Friends," the police chief began. "Today I have a sad obligation."

The villagers abandoned their conversations and

crowded in like sheep to brace themselves. A covered cart was beside the mounted men in the road.

Capitán Fermín did not dare look at Señora Clara, who was already tearing at her hair and wailing. Nor did he even try to stop Sonia from walking unsteadily to the cart when she spotted the worn sole of a familiar thick-heeled shoe.

She pulled back the canvas. Black flies buzzed at Luis's eyes, half opened and fixed on her in accusation. Thieves had turned his hip pockets out. His thick hair was matted with blood where their bullets had blasted through his skull.

"I thought it was a dead animal on the tracks," Marco told the stunned crowd.

He had managed to stop his fine train just in time.

CHAPTER 2

A Revelation

IT WAS SONIA who washed the bruises on Luis's face because Señora Clara could not. It was Sonia who combed his thick hair down around his wounds. Sonia who knotted his tie and folded his stiffened hands. When she was through, she sat staring mutely at her friend's body, ashamed at how she had failed him so completely.

Weeks later, when other girls could dream again of boys holding their hands by the river, Sonia could not close her eyes without seeing images of Luis's body laid out like a doll on his kitchen table. She could still see the worn cuff on his trousers and the plain wooden coffin bobbing on men's shoulders through the trees. She conjured faceless men and the sound of their bullets tearing through his skull for a few miserable coins. Finally, she decided to stop sleeping altogether.

"The girl is sick with sorrow," Blanca explained to the women who stopped by to inquire. There was talk at the market that Sonia's eyes had become dull, that she refused to stir from her room.

"It was the mother's fault," Sonia heard one say. "I'm sure of it. An evil secret Clara is being punished for. Your poor child could do nothing."

Sonia turned over in her bed. *Where was God in all of this?* she wondered bitterly. Why had he turned a deaf ear to her supplications for Luis? Priests could spin long sermons on the topic of God's mysterious ways, but it made no sense to her at all. In fact, it made her furious. Never once had she complained of her fate. She'd shouldered everything that had been expected of her. She'd prayed each night without fail, each *milagro* like a bead in an endless rosary.

And yet Luis had still died—and now his mother was being blamed.

A knot of doubt squeezed inside her for the first time in her life. It all seemed to grow clear now. She had held Luis in her heart with all her might—and he'd still been murdered. What if she had no power, no magic or special favor? What if all there was in the world was luck?

Sonia sat up slowly and stared at her shawl, which was

hanging near her door. It all made sense now. Her whole life had been built around a silly mountain myth. She was nothing but a fraud, a girl in a costume. She was as helpless as anyone else in Tres Montes.

"So, are you going to waste away here forever?" Tía Neli had appeared at her bedside with a cup of hot tea. "I can't take much more of these nosy visitors."

"Send them away," Sonia mumbled.

"I've tried, but no one takes a hint in this town." She sat at the edge of Sonia's bed and held out the cup. "Drink this. I put special pepper in it."

Sonia stared into her aunt's bright eyes instead. Tía Neli had always loved her dearly, having no daughters of her own. "I'm serious, Tía. Send them away. Then tell them I can't give them what they all want."

Tía Neli put a hand to Sonia's forehead and set down the tea. "Every sadness passes, you know. Even a terrible one like this."

Sonia shook her head, her eyes brimming with tears. "It's not only sadness, Tía. It's more than that. I *can't do* what everyone wants. I can't stop bad times from finding us. I can't control things any more than they can."

Tía Neli flinched, and Sonia knew that her aunt had been thinking of Luis, too—and adding up the facts.

"Does it matter?" she said. "I've lived in Tres Montes long enough to know it's pointless to terrify a mountainside of people with unpleasant realities—which are never welcomed, anyway. Maybe it's honorable enough to give elders hope in their old age. Besides, any god would say it's a sin to make your parents suffer with worry."

But for once Sonia would not be agreeable. "And what of my suffering? Do you know what it's like to live as I do? To be asked to make rain in the dry season? To cure coughs? To dress your dead friend because you couldn't save him? And *why* am I cursed this way? Because I was born on the wrong night, that's all. It's all been a silly lie!"

"Shhh!" Tía Neli bit her lip and walked to the window to check the yard.

"I need you to help me," Sonia insisted. "I've wandered around town like an armadillo long enough. I need you to help me tell everyone the truth."

But Tía Neli only turned and put up her hand. "Your *abuela* used to say, 'God often does the right thing by crooked means.' You have to be patient. A solution will present itself."

Tears of frustration spilled from Sonia's eyes. "I can't trust God! He's abandoned me completely!"

"Don't talk nonsense." Tía Neli nodded to the ladies who had finally left along the path. She turned to Sonia with a stern face. "It's time to get up. The kitchen floor needs sweeping."

Sonia stared at her hopelessly.

"Go," Tía Neli said firmly. "Go, and leave the rest to me."

CHAPTER 3
Tía Neli's News

A FEW DAYS later, Sonia had just finished her honey toast and coffee when she heard a pounding on the door. It was Tía Neli, breathless with excitement to announce the big news. The rancher's daughter, Cuca, who lived farther up the mountain, had broken her hand in a careless fall from her horse. Tía Neli had been visiting the girl's mother when it happened. She'd heard the bones snap like twigs. She'd seen the girl's hand inflate like a frog's throat in springtime.

"She can't travel to the capital this year!" Tía Neli cried gleefully. "She'll be useless as a worker! Isn't that fantastic!"

Sonia gave her aunt a blank look.

Tía Neli stopped in her tracks and grabbed her niece's hands. "I've been puzzling for days for a way to help you without disturbing matters too much," she said. "Don't you see? This is the answer! This is your chance to be free of your troubles and still make your parents proud—or at least richer, if you're smart. Run—find your father!"

Sonia had no real idea of what her aunt was talking about, but she rushed down the path to the vegetable garden. Felix was crouched over a tender squash vine, too deaf to hear his daughter calling him.

"Papi," she said, reaching for his elbow. But just as she spoke, Sonia felt a gust of winter wind and something falling away from her, dropping as softly as a silk ribbon from her long, black hair. She looked all around—so shocking was the feeling!—but saw nothing.

It was only as she stood panting in front of her startled father that she began to collect her thoughts. Somewhere on the path between Tía Neli and her father, the ties that bound her to their home in Tres Montes had been cut loose.

"Come," she said, shaking. "There is important news at the house."

By the time Felix and Sonia arrived, the rest of family was already gathered. Blanca was softening beans, Tía Neli was pacing, and Rafael, home early from his weekend card game, was pretending to nap on the couch. Sonia moved his feet and sat down beside him to listen.

25

As a courtesy to his know-it-all sister, Felix let Tía Neli share her news between sips of her coffee. Naturally, he was not happy in the least with his sister's bold interference in Sonia's life. He often said Neli's longing for all modern things was repellent, that she was never satisfied with the simple beauty of a mountain life, and her son, Pedro, was plagued by the same ailment. With his silly mother's blessings, the boy had left three years earlier to slaughter hogs somewhere in the North.

"Turn your nose up if you like, but it's thanks to Pedro's hogs that I have my house," Tía Neli always bragged. But Felix still scoffed at her new shoes and the perfume she wore even to water the goats' trough. He thanked God every day that Blanca had shown no such inclination.

Felix followed the bread crumbs to where Tía Neli's story was leading. When she finished, he crossed his arms and gave her an annoyed look.

"My children are staying put, Sister," he said firmly.

"But, Felix, Sonia can go to the capital instead of Cuca and learn a skill. She'll see something besides cows and pine trees. Imagine it: the capital—a big city." She pursed her lips and gave Sonia an especially pained look. "Besides, look at her: The girl needs a bit of rest from all these unpleasant shocks. Her eyes looked bruised from worry. Have pity!"

"She'll rest here just fine in her own bed."

"Well, then, how about the money? Or is it that you don't mind eating only beans every day?"

Sonia sat on the edge of her seat barely breathing as Tía Neli made her case. Escaping as a worker in the capital! She had once seen a picture of the domes of the presidential palace. A few of the older girls from school worked there each winter, far away from their parents and mountain ways. Now maybe Sonia would have a chance to see it herself—and escape from her worries. She gave Rafael a pleading glance for help.

He tapped Sonia gently with his toes and propped himself up. "If I know Sonia, she'll find a way to earn more money than Papi and me!" he said, giving her braid a tug.

Felix shot him an angry look. "It's too dangerous for an innocent girl to be alone in the city," he said. "Think of her on the trolley. Those savages might steal your sister off or pinch her raw."

"Modern women learn how to take care of themselves, Brother," Tía Neli argued. "And if she works in a good house, the owner will invest in her safety. I've heard they post guards everywhere on those estates." She turned to her niece, unable to resist dropping a morsel to cheer her. "You might travel in a fancy car with a driver!"

Sonia's eyes grew wide. "A chauffeur?"

"What kind of car?" Rafael asked.

"Who *cares* about cars?" Felix snapped. "Sonia Ocampo a servant? Ridiculous! She's a gift from God."

"So what? Everyone needs to know about a little dusting and fetching—even an angel," Tía Neli insisted. "How do you think heaven stays so white and clean? Anyway, I promise you, she'll be in a reputable house. We'll arrange for her to go with Ramona. She'll make sure her girls treat Sonia like a sister." Here she paused carefully. "In return, Sonia will bless and protect them. Isn't that right, *niña*?"

Sonia stared at her aunt. "Of course."

"And who'll protect us right here, eh?" Felix stabbed the table with his forefinger. "The rainy season is practically upon us, Neli. Storms, illness—where will we be without her?"

The mere thought of an entire season of new petitions drove Sonia to near madness. Reading her expression, Rafael chimed in.

"In that case, lend *me* one of her dresses," he offered. "I'm nearly twenty, and I have nice legs. I'll be happy to go in her place and earn all the money."

"*¡Silencio!*" ordered Felix.

Tía Neli bit her lip to keep from laughing and shook her finger at her brother. "Don't be such a brute, Felix. God has sent this chance to Sonia for a reason. It would be rude of you to ignore it. Besides, why do we have children, *hermano*, if it is not to help us when we get old? She's young and strong and able to work."

She looked around the shabby kitchen.

"It's time to get our noses out from the clouds and put our feet on firm ground. A new stove is in order, and you won't last much longer in the mines to save enough for that. Haven't you seen the shape Guacho's in after twenty-five years in the mine?"

Felix grimaced and looked away from Blanca. He knew she deserved better.

For an agonizing moment, Sonia thought her father would once again refuse. Hope shriveled in her chest. One way or another, she had to be free. She would have to be bold in dealing with her father. There was only one voice of authority that no traditional man could ignore. It was even stronger than God's.

She went to her father and pressed his hand to her cheek, hoping he would not detect the daring lie that had gathered on her lips. Felix Ocampo had always prided himself on being an obedient son. He'd even honored his mother's dying wish to be buried with a cup of tea in one hand and her favorite knitting needles in the other. Sonia leaned in close to his ear.

"Papi, I had a vision. Abuela came to me last night and

told me to leave Tres Montes. I didn't want to frighten you, but now I have no choice."

Her father's eyebrows shot up in surprise. "My mother?" he exclaimed. "She came to you?" Everyone knew that the dead bothered themselves only with the most important things.

"Yes. Abuela said, 'Go on, *mi vida*. There is a place for you in the city.' This job is what she must have meant."

Tía Neli arched her brow and nervously reached for her necklace.

"Mamá was always wise. . . ." she offered cautiously. "That's where I get my brains."

Sonia knelt near her father and looked into his worried eyes. "I know you want me here in Tres Montes. But Tía and Abuela are right. This work will help us with the things we need. God has presented this chance for a reason."

"January through September." Tía Neli counted on her fingers. "Nine months. She'll be home in no time."

Blanca turned from her pot at last and regarded Sonia carefully. Sonia knew that her mother loved her children above all else and found it nearly impossible to see them suffer. She could see that no amount of tea and incense had helped chase away the nightmares. Blanca glanced over her shoulder into the scant pot of beans that would have to stretch to feed the entire family. Only one thing frightened a mother in Tres Montes more than starving.

"They never come back the same," she said quietly.

"Blanca—" Tía Neli began.

"You know it's true, Neli. I am not a modern woman like you, but I'm not a stupid one, either. The young go places we can hardly imagine, but they come back with new words in their mouths and new ways in their hearts. They learn to look at their own parents with shame. Suddenly Tres Montes is too slow for them, too small, too dusty and poor. They hate to come home, and then, one day, they forget their own families altogether. We lose them forever."

A long silence fell on the Ocampos. Even Tía Neli sighed, lost in thoughts of whether Pedro would wrap her legs in warm blankets one day when she got old.

It was Rafael who rescued them. He forced a smile over his sad eyes and clapped his hands twice.

"¡Vamos! We've had enough wakes," he chided. "It's time to be happy again. I say, Abuela is right. If Sonia has the chance to work in the capital, she should go and not look back." He turned to his sister and winked. "Just make sure you come back with lots of money, Sonia. I could use a new truck."

"Finally! Someone has good sense!" Tía Neli patted

her lips with a napkin and took Felix's hand. "I will arrange to see Arenas in a few days. He's hiring the last round of workers for the season next week. She'll make you proud. You'll see."

"I am already proud," Felix muttered. Then he looked at his wife and did the unthinkable. "*Bueno*, Blanca. You nursed her yourself. What do we do with the girl?"

Sonia squirmed in her chair as her mother turned back to look at her.

Then Blanca lowered her eyes and spoke loudly enough for Felix to hear. Her words rang out like a proclamation, though tears were already pooled in her eyes.

"Tell Abuela to be still in her grave. There is no stopping a girl born stronger than the wind. Let Sonia go."

CHAPTER 4
A Deal with Señor Arenas

SONIA GLANCED DOWN at her feet as she trudged down the steep incline toward the plaza below. She had been traveling down the hillside for only a short time, but her boots were already consumed in the yellow dust that would hover in Tres Montes for the duration of the dry season. The thin powder floated in the air and made everything look faded. Even the girls walking just ahead of her looked like floating spirits.

In the weak morning sunlight, and still so far away, the plaza looked deserted. The main street was long and narrow, lined with flat-topped stucco buildings and windows dressed in rusty iron bars. Their large hand-painted letters marked each establishment. FARMACIA, POLICÍA, REGISTRO CIVIL. From there, small winding roads spread out haphazardly and ended at the church ruins. Sonia looked away, hoping that today might be her chance to leave it all behind.

She felt in her pocket for her birth registration, her money, and her handkerchief; everything was in order. For now, it was only her boots that were the problem. She would have to make them shine like glass before they met Señor Arenas. Tía Neli, who had assigned herself chaperone, would insist. After all, she had made it clear how important it was to make a good impression.

"To serve a fine family in a big city, you must be impeccable in your appearance and manners," her aunt had told her. "One has to be a person who cares about the smallest details." Even silly ones, Sonia assumed, like dusty boots.

As the girls finally reached the valley, they rushed to get the taxi drivers' attention, negotiating for a proper price. Tía Neli surveyed the confusion calmly.

"You!" She snapped her fingers at the back of a young man with a bike taxi at the edge of the highway. He tossed away his drink, beamed a smile, and pedaled toward them.

To Sonia's surprise, it was Pancho Muñoz, from school. She lowered her shawl to greet him, her heart already racing.

"What luck that it's you," she said politely over the squeaks of his rusty wheels. He had only recently begun his job, but already Pancho looked like the other taxi boys. He seemed taller in the pressed blue shirt of a taxi apprentice, much older than he did in his worn cotton shirts and bare feet during the week at school, when he was nothing more than Pancho the Orphan about whom the other girls snickered. He was too formal when he spoke, they said, too given to daydreams. But Sonia liked him for all of those qualities. Now, in the sunshine, he looked especially handsome.

Pancho tipped his cap, blushing. "We've missed you at school, Sonia. I hope you're feeling better."

Sonia went mute in his gaze. For one thing, he had sweet brown eyes. But there was also no explanation she could give for avoiding everyone. The wind gusted sharply again, and Tía Neli nudged her forward. "We'll be late," she announced.

Pancho offered Sonia his hand and cast an appreciative glance at her legs as she climbed onto the bench.

Tía Neli frowned at him and settled in beside her niece.

"To the plaza, *por favor*." She leaned in to Sonia, who was already at work on her boots. "I'll do the talking from here."

The office was small and hot. Girls waiting for interviews filled every seat in the hallway. Sonia wiped the perspiration from her lip and peered over her aunt's shoulder as they read the job listings provided.

Today Señor Arenas was hiring for several employers. A glass factory in the west was looking for steady-handed workers and a citrus farm to the south wanted workers who didn't whine about red ants or scorching heat. A few nannies were needed to tend to the imperial children of dignitaries. But Tía Neli pointed at the last entry. It was only two words: Casa Masón. "That's the one," she whispered. "Wait here."

She walked over to the young secretary toiling behind an old desk. "How many are needed at Casa Masón?" she asked.

The secretary stopped typing and looked up crossly over the top of her glasses. She opened a coffee-stained folder and glanced at the last page.

"Four in total for the widow," she said primly. "But don't get your hopes up, *señora*. We take only experienced girls for such a position." She tossed Sonia a dubious glance. "Our client is very clear on that point."

Tía Neli walked back to her seat and patted Sonía's hand.

"Change that face, *niña*," she said firmly. "You'll be fine. It's all in how you handle these silly men."

❖ ❖ ❖

"How do I know she'll be any good?" Señor Arenas asked as he leaned back in his chair and folded his hands over his protruding belly. He scrutinized Sonia as a rancher might eye one of his herd. "She looks a bit scrawny. I've got fifty other girls to chose from who are meatier and experienced." Sonia knew it was true. As always there were more girls than he could possibly hire—a tidy situation for a businessman with the only legal employment agency for a hundred miles.

Tía Neli smiled and waved her hand in the air as if shooing a pesky fly.

"You have fifty very ordinary girls, *señor*. What I'm offering you is an *extraordinary* one."

Sonia nudged Tía Neli with her heel, hoping to silence her discretely. She longed to be ordinary, nothing more. Sonia tried her best to smile and ignore the perspiration running down her back.

Señor Arenas twirled a toothpick and shrugged. "She's pretty enough," he said. "I'll give you that."

"Of course she is. And she has a natural elegance, *señor*, She was born with it. If that's not extraordinary, I don't know what is!"

Señor Arenas clamped his gold-rimmed teeth down on a toothpick. "But can she work?"

Tía Neli gave him a pout and shook her head. "Really,

Señor Arenas, it's as though you'd never heard of the Ocampos. We are a most hardworking and revered family, as you know. *This* is the girl everyone has heard of: Sonia, the girl who silenced the winds of Tres Montes." She laid Sonia's shawl across his desk to show him the *milagros* as proof. "Ask your mother. She comes to Sonia for petitions from time to time."

"Tía—" Sonia began in protest.

But Señor Arenas had already pushed the garment away in disgust. "Please! Enough with old superstitions! This is the capital we're talking about. Nobody there cares about that. In fact, my girls are on strict orders not to talk such nonsense at their jobs! It makes us sound like lunatics. I don't need girls who think they're angels. What *I* need, *señora*, are girls who know their place, girls who can work like brutes without anyone knowing they're in the room."

Tía Neli's face reddened. "Well, in any case, it doesn't matter," she said, taking her niece's hands. "Show Señor Arenas your hands, Sonia. You'll notice, *señor*, that her hands are slender but strong—perfect for doing the meticulous work you need in a fine household. They seem to me the same hands of a future pastry chef. If you ask me, she'd make a marvelous kitchen apprentice."

Sonia glanced down and almost gasped. Her aunt had

given her three large bills, wrapped in a rubber band. It was enough to buy food for a month. Tía Neli nodded sweetly in Señor Arenas's direction.

Sonia drew her hands from her lap and extended them, palms down for inspection, though she couldn't think of where to look in her embarrassment. She turned her gaze to the waiting area, where the remaining girls waited hopefully for their chance at work contracts.

Immediately, she felt Señor Arenas's hands caress her wrists. When he withdrew, the bills were tucked between his own stubby fingers. He slipped them inside his shirt pocket casually.

"Pastry chef." He chuckled.

He opened a file folder and slid on his dirty glasses. After a few moments, he made a whistling sound to summon the secretary.

"Send the rest home."

The secretary cast an insulted look at Sonia as she turned to go inform the others. Sonia tried to look innocent, but she knew she had cheated. What kind of girl bribed her way ahead of friends and neighbors?

It's your only chance, she told herself. *It's your only escape.*

Señor Arenas offered her a form for her signature. "You do know how to write, don't you?"

Sonia nodded and studied the paperwork. Her name had been added to a list of three others under a column marked CASA MASÓN.

Señor Arenas reached into his drawer and pulled out a pretty spice bottle. He placed it before her on his desk. The foil label read ESPECIAS MASÓN.

"So you know where you're going," he said, tapping the lid. "Casa Masón spices are known the world over. It's the old widow Katarina Masón who runs the business now, of course. She's rich beyond all your dreams since her husband died. Take care to please her, *niña*. Opportunities like this don't come often, understand? A hundred other girls would die to have your spot." He pointed at the shawl in her lap. "And make sure you leave *that* thing behind."

"Gladly, *señor*!" Sonia answered, and signed her name.

"Congratulations," a jobless girl called to Sonia as they left the building.

"Good luck comes to those who are worthy," cried another.

Sonia looked back and nodded silently, her mouth glued with shame.

Tía Neli patted her back as they climbed into a taxi to take them all the way home in celebration. She held the jar under her nose to sniff the faded scent of all corners of the world.

"We did it! My very own niece working with one of the richest families in the whole country! Imagine it! Inside Casa Masón! I know you won't forget what I've done for you, Sonia." Her eyes were already dreamy with ideas.

CHAPTER 5
Escuelita

SONIA EXPECTED TO find Abuela's spirit waiting at the edge of her bed to scold her for brazen lies and bribery. When her grandmother was cross, she pulled off people's covers or rattled at their windows to keep them awake. Once she'd flattened all of Rafael's tires for forgetting to bring her daisies on the anniversary of her death.

But the house had stayed calm all night.

"Looks like you're safe, *hermanita*," Rafael told her across the kitchen table at breakfast. "Abuela always had good sense. Even she knows you made the right decision."

Sonia stared into her porridge guiltily. "Well, I might have exaggerated a little."

Rafael's eyebrows shot up in proud surprise. His mouth dropped open as he laughed in disbelief. "And they say *I'm* reckless!"

"*Ay, por favor,* Rafael. You spend your whole life telling white lies to Papi."

"True enough," he admitted. "Just watch your step, though. Abuela was never one to let things slide."

Felix blared the horn, calling Rafael to work.

Sonia left for school, whistling replies to the birds along the way and trying to feel happy. It was bad enough to have lied, but there was one regret she hadn't confessed to anyone.

Pancho.

How would she tell him?

She'd found herself thinking of him since the taxi ride. They had suffered together for years inside the one-room building, listening to the monotony of Irina Gomez's voice. Both were basically friendless — Sonia, because the other girls were afraid she already knew their secrets, and besides, she was too important to befriend, and Pancho because he was not important enough. He had no parents to protect him, no last name that mattered. He was simply an orphan who had found a roof over his head thanks to the kind help of Señor Pasqual, whose wife had a soft heart for abandoned cats and boys.

She thought of all the times he'd regaled her with stories composed during lonely nights lying on the floor of his employer's kitchen. She liked that he had dreams in his head, beyond stealing kisses or getting drunk. She liked how his stories left her hopeful when they were finished.

"You'll be a poet one day," she'd told him. "You can recite them for the president. I bet he'll give you a medal."

Pancho had only smiled in his typical close-lipped way. "I'd rather recite them for you," he'd said.

It made her secretly love him on the spot, though neither of them had ever spoken such things. What was the point? Rafael could dally with any girl he pleased, but Felix placed a whole other set of limitations on his virtuous daughter. No blouses that might hint at her curves. No modern hairdos or lipstick, however pale. No boys, period. Still, Sonia found herself thinking of Pancho often.

She glanced nervously around the school grounds, trying to decide if she felt more relieved or disappointed to find Pancho missing. A tangle of girls her age under the acacia tree caught her attention. They were gossiping as always, and if she wasn't imagining things, glancing in her direction.

She was about to join them when, as if materializing from her thoughts, Pancho stepped out of the shadows. "Is it true what people are saying?" he asked.

Sonia jumped in surprise. "*Por Dios*, Pancho! You frightened me." He was wearing his old clothes again, his pants patched at the knees. Still, his legs were muscular, and he'd grown almost as tall as Rafael. His voice was low and even.

"Forgive me."

"You shouldn't stalk like a panther!"

He bowed his head and took a step closer than he had ever dared before. Standing this close, she noticed his long eyelashes, the green specks in his eyes, and how the corners of his mouth were turned down the way they did when Irina Gomez ignored his raised hand. His expression looked darker than she ever remembered.

"You haven't answered me, though. Are you leaving with Ramona's girls?" he asked. "To the capital?"

Sonia chewed her lip, already feeling the sting of his hurt. "I was going to tell you, Pancho."

"Oh." He studied his dusty feet.

She shifted uneasily. His closeness made her stomach lurch in a way that was thrilling and terrifying all at once.

"It's just that I can't stay here, Pancho," she said at last.

Pancho's fingertips brushed against hers. "Why not? Your family is here, your friends." He lowered his voice to a whisper. "The people who love you."

Sonia did not dare move an inch as he raised his eyes to hers. Pancho had no idea she was a fraud, she thought. A boy like this deserved more than lies.

"Please don't ask me to explain why I'm leaving, Pancho."

"But, Sonia—" He reached for her hand and pulled her closer still.

Suddenly, the school bell rang out. Irina Gomez frowned in their direction.

"Let's go," Sonia said quickly, pulling free. "We'll be late."

It was a well-known fact that Irina Gomez despised her students. In her opinion, the younger ones were unruly and talkative, and the older ones disappeared for distant jobs whenever the opportunity presented itself. As a result, no one knew much of anything that she, "the most promising student of pedagogy at the university," tried to teach them.

When she announced their failing grades from her record book, she was fond of saying, "With scores like these, you will be laborers. Nothing more. We all have a place in life."

"Ignore her," Rafael said whenever Sonia complained about the teacher's dreariness. He'd left the teacher and her pronouncements behind forever two years earlier. "Irina Gomez has never known passion in her heart, mind, or loins. How can she fan a flame of hope in anyone else?"

Sonia found her seat and looked around for what she knew would be the last time. Then someone slipped in beside her and tapped her on the shoulder.

Eva Catá had round blue eyes and glossy lips. She was the ambassador of the older girls and a regular employee of Casa Masón. A pleasant scent of rosewater and talcum powder lingered all around her.

"*Ay*, dear Sonia. Is it true? Are you coming with us this year?" Eva, whose mother arranged successful marriages all over the mountainside, prided herself on keeping current on everyone's personal affairs.

The village, it seemed, was shocked by the news of her upcoming departure. She was as much a part of the mountain as the metals that formed in its belly. Everyone was buzzing with the news.

"Yes," Sonia said, motioning toward the girl with a bandaged hand. "Cuca was hurt by her horse."

Eva clapped.

"Sonia Ocampo coming with us! I can scarcely believe it! What a blessing—although we'll miss Cuca, naturally!"

"I hope I'll be a help," Sonia said cautiously. She noticed other girls watching and listening to their conversation.

"I have no doubt at all. And just wait until you see the

estate; it's a mansion. And, in case you don't know, the city is full of handsome workers."

Sonia's eyes flitted to Pancho; she hoped he had not heard. He had found his seat and was at least pretending not to listen from his spot ahead of Sonia.

Eva followed the look in an instant. She reached over and blew on Pancho's neck.

"Then again, I suspect some handsome boys here will miss you, too."

She walked back to her seat at the rear, unconcerned by Pancho's shame burning through the air.

Irina Gomez took her place beneath the crooked portrait of the president and opened her lesson book.

"Wait for me after school," Pancho whispered over his shoulder. "I have something important to tell you."

Sonia looked over the top of her book curiously. "What is it?"

He did not reply. Sonia nudged his back with the tip of her eraser. "Tell me."

He turned his head slowly and lifted his grave eyes. "I wanted to tell you myself," he said a little pointedly. "I, too, am leaving school. This is my final day."

Sonia's eyes widened, and she leaned forward. "What are you saying?"

He turned completely in his chair. "Señor Pasqual

thinks I would make a fine taxi boy. I've got strong legs, and I've apprenticed long enough on weekends to make a good salary. Who knows? One day I might take over his business. There's nothing here for me anymore. I've learned as much as Irina Gomez will ever be able to teach me."

Sonia felt her teacher's icy stare. The room had fallen silent all around them.

"Is that so?" Irina Gomez said, eyeing Pancho critically. "Well, I certainly haven't been able to teach you to be quiet, have I? Get to work."

Giggles erupted from the back row. Pancho's whole face burned brightly as he bowed his head in apology and turned back to his lessons.

Sonia bent over her book, but soon she was daydreaming while gazing at the portrait above her teacher's head. *No more schooling, Pancho? What about your dream of becoming a poet for* el presidente? she wanted to ask him. She knew he liked to read and learn as much as she did. *What about the poems you long to write?*

But she never got the chance. In the afternoon Irina Gomez gave her a long lecture about venturing on as a decent young woman among city vipers. When she dismissed Sonia at last, Eva was waiting outside. She grabbed Sonia by the arm for the first time in her life, chattering excitedly about their plans for the trip and the farewell party that would be held in her honor that evening. Sonia listened as if in a happy dream. She forgot all about Pancho, who waited for her loyally in the deep shade of their favorite reading tree.

It was when she was putting away her tattered schoolbooks later that she realized her thoughtlessness. She tried not to think of his serious eyes, the formal way he held back his shoulders when they spoke, and the funny stories he had always invented simply to amuse her. Their friendship would never have blossomed into anything more—thanks to the watchful eye of her father, she reasoned. Besides, as much as she wanted to apologize, she knew it would be wrong to lie about why she was leaving.

Forgive me for keeping secrets, Pancho, she thought glumly. *But it's for the best this way.*

CHAPTER 6
Adiós, Tres Montes

THE CLEARING BEHIND Sonia's house blazed with a bon-
fire, and tree branches were strung with tin-can lanterns
that illuminated the long table laden with treats. Pork
tamales and vegetables would accompany the chickens
and hogs that were roasting on coals nearby.

The old miners were singing as her father plucked on
his guitar. The varnish had worn away, but the sound was
still lovely. He led the men in an old rhyme as their wives
joined them, clapping and laughing behind their backs.

> *Mi papá se fue al puerto y me dejo una navaja,*
> *con un letrero que dice, "Si quieres comer, trabaja."*

> *My father went to the harbor and he left me a carved*
> *knife —*

Sonia wandered along the table and hummed the last line: "If you want to eat, then you'll have to work in this life."

Excitement left her with no appetite. She nibbled on a meat pie and tried to make polite conversation, but all the while she watched from the corner of her eye for Pancho, who had not arrived.

All their other neighbors had come with heartfelt good-byes and carnations to throw at her feet.

"I promise you that she will carry your prayers on her journey," Blanca assured them as she collected the tiny metal shapes in a pouch that the tanner had made especially for the occasion. Sonia barely looked at them.

"What will we do without you?" asked Inez, rubbing her sore knees. The rancher's wife had been bent in prayer over exaggerated confessions at the church ruins since her daughter's accident. Cuca stood beside her wearing her bandage mitten, damning proof of some supposed hidden guilt.

"We've had too many tears these days, Inez," Tía Neli said kindly. "Tonight is a night to forget. Bad times, happy face; let's try to celebrate."

Cuca stepped forward and kissed Sonia on each cheek. "We'll be counting the days until God brings you home."

"Thank you." Sonia pointed at Cuca's mitten. "Does it hurt very much?"

Cuca shrugged. "Not too much anymore. But here—" She reached into her pocket and pulled out a tattered map. "I've brought a present for you. It's the capital."

Sonia studied the streets and squiggles. It was hard to imagine herself in a place so large. There were train stations and hospitals, a university and a grid of streets with impressive names.

"What does X mean?" she asked. A large section of streets were crossed off.

"The slum." Cuca shook her head and whispered. "Don't find yourself there."

Inez turned from Tía Neli and reached out for Sonia's hand.

"Won't you say a prayer for us to be safe until your return?" she asked.

Before Sonia could refuse, the women huddled close and joined hands. Sonia bowed her head, but she did not pray. Instead she let her mind wander to the grid of winding streets. It was hard to believe that this would be her last night in Tres Montes—at least for a long while. As much as she wanted to go to the capital, she knew she'd miss the things she loved: the start of the rains, the bullfrogs clinging to the walls, napping to the sound of rain hitting the roof. Nine months suddenly seemed an eternity to be without her parents, Rafael, and Tía Neli. It was also long enough, she realized, for someone like Pancho to forget her entirely. *Where on earth could he be?* she wondered.

When she was sure that enough time had passed for a prayer, she opened her eyes.

"All will be well," she mumbled. "Good rains, good crops, good health."

"There you are, *amorcito!*" Eva was radiant in a white cotton dress that skimmed her caramel shoulders.

"You should be dancing!" she said, linking her arm through Sonia's. "It's a party, after all." She lowered her voice to a whisper as she led Sonia away. "It's all right, isn't it? Magic girls can dance?"

Sonia smiled. "Let's find Rafael."

Girls were huddled around Tía Neli's record player, a gift from Pedro, along with music he'd bought on one of his work trips. Several girls danced together, arguing over leading; a few swayed with their sleepy siblings on their hips. Rafael, the lone rooster in the henhouse, gave each girl a turn at dancing, his eyes glassy with pleasure. Finally, he saw his baby sister watching him.

"Sonia!" he called.

He pulled her out to dance as everyone around them clapped and hooted. Rafael was handsome, even with his hair disheveled and his shirttails hanging over his jeans. He was a wonderful dancer, so completely free and sure with all his movements that he made Sonia feel brave in her own clumsier rhythms. She could feel the envious stares of the crowd watching them, but for once she didn't mind people's eyes on her. She felt free and proud with Rafael.

"You're the big breadwinner in the family now!" he said, twirling her dramatically. "Thank God it doesn't have to be me!" He planted an enormous kiss on Sonia's cheek. "I've decided I'm meant to be a man of leisure."

"And who's going to maintain you? One of your girlfriends? Or should I say, one of your *friend's* girlfriends?" Sonia teased.

Rafael pretended to look hurt. "Who are you calling a gigolo? Someone has to keep the ladies from going crazy without their men. But don't worry, *hermanita*. I'm an honorable guy. Ask them: we're talking and dancing— that's all. Most of the time, anyway."

"Tell that to their boyfriends when they come back from their jobs. They'll be looking for you!"

Rafael threw his head back and laughed as they circled the dance area. "They'll never catch me!"

When the music ended, the crowd burst into applause. Rafael took her face in his hands and suddenly grew serious. "I'm going to miss you, Sonia. Take care of yourself."

She rested her forehead on his chin and took in the smell of beer and his sweet aftershave. "Walk me back to the house, will you?" She pointed at the dark path that led home. "I have to finish packing."

A groan of disappointment lifted as they started toward the path. They had not gone two steps when someone called to them.

"Where are you going, Rafael? It's still early."

Sonia bristled at the sound of another girl's voice. She had no interest in sharing her brother with one of his silly girlfriends tonight.

When she turned, she saw it was Dalia. Older than Sonia, she knew how to reduce boys to quivers with only her eyes, even Rafael. She had grown up alongside brothers, who were always in one kind of trouble or another. As a result, she could drown an unwanted litter of kittens without mercy and shoot the buttons off a man's shirt at a distance of thirty paces. Of all the people Sonia had ever known, only Dalia had never approached for prayers. She had never asked God or anyone else for so much as a hairpin. Dalia would be leaving for Casa Masón tomorrow as well.

Sonia held tightly to her brother's hand as Rafael paused.

"Talk to her later," she whispered.

Rafael sighed. "But, *mamita*, she's got all those curves, and here I am with no brakes. . . ."

"Let's go."

But Rafael did not budge. He and Dalia kept staring at each other as if an entire unspoken conversation were unfolding.

"Don't go," Dalia said finally. "Please."

"I have to, *linda*," he said gently. "Now, be good, and keep your promises."

He blew Dalia a kiss and turned away.

"What was that all about?" Sonia asked.

He slung his arm around her shoulder. They walked in silence toward the house.

Sonia had always hated darkness. At night white cows sometimes wandered away from their pens and frightened her with glowing eyes and groans at her window.

"Calm yourself," Rafael would tell her when she was afraid. "The darkness can hold good surprises, too. Think of gold in the mines."

When they reached their room, Rafael lay back on his narrow bed to stare at the ceiling. Sonia began folding the last of her things into her trunk. The train to the capital would leave the following day. She surveyed the last of her belongings. Tía Neli had offered a greasy balm for chapped hands, and (in secret) a nearly new pair of shoes in case she had somewhere fancy to go with a companion. Her father had presented her with pressed wildflowers to remember the patch outside her window. Blanca had packed food for the journey.

"What is it, Rafael?" Sonia asked. "You're too quiet."

"Hmm?"

"Are you mad that it's me who is leaving?"

Rafael sat up and smiled at her tenderly. "How can I be jealous when something good happens to my little sister? If it is good for you, I'm happy. You're doing what you want to do."

Sonia looked into her hands.

"You do want to go, don't you?" he asked.

"Of course," she said. "I'm just . . . nervous. The capital is a big place."

"*Ay*, you're like a bean. The first sight of boiling water, and you shrivel up in fear! I liked you better as an angel."

"I hate it when you make fun of me."

Rafael smiled and ran his fingers through his hair.

"Hide the fear away in your pocket, will you?" he said. "What would you do here in Tres Montes, Sonia?

We both know that not even a magic girl can fill stomachs with wind and spells. I love Papi, but he is completely wrong. Young people like us, we need more. Money, opportunities . . ."

This was why she loved Rafael so dearly. He was the only one who told her the truth, the only one from whom she kept no secrets.

"I'll send as much money as I can," she said earnestly. "Every penny that I don't need. We'll save for your truck."

Rafael began to speak, but then seemed lost in thought once again.

"What?" she asked.

"*Nada, nada.*"

"Tell me," she said, crossing to his bed. "You can't hide things from me, remember?"

He stood and peered out the window. "You will swear to silence? If not, I'll find you and cut out your tongue," he warned.

Sonia rolled her eyes at his threat. They never told each other's transgressions, although it was usually Sonia making excuses for why Rafael—often out carousing all night—was sleeping late.

"How gallant of you to threaten a lady," she said. "Say it, already. You know I'll keep my word."

He leaned in and whispered in her ear.

"I *am* leaving."

Sonia paused and arched her brow. It was impossible. The few men's work permits were all gone now. The boys lucky enough to get one from Señor Arenas had left a month earlier; their lonely girlfriends had been at the party.

"Liar."

Rafael looked into her face earnestly and waited. Slowly, she realized his meaning. She thought at once of Luis in his clean shirt and tie. Her stomach sank to her shoes. "*Por Dios*, don't do something stupid."

"Since when is making money stupid? In a few months, I'll earn what it would take me years to earn in the mines."

"It's not the money! Luis died trying to make that crossing—just to find work."

"There are lots of ways to die," he said quietly. "A mine can kill you, too."

"And what about bandits, Rafael? Or worse, the border guards? They don't care who they shoot."

"They're lousy shots."

"Be serious!"

"It's serious you want?" His face looked hard in a way that it almost never did. "Then here it is: I have no choice but to take the risk. What happens when Papi can't work the mines? Then it's up to me to feed us all. I don't want to

60

live my life like him, crawling through caves and coughing up dust while somebody else gets rich."

"He'll never let you go."

"He won't have a choice. I'll be halfway there by the time he realizes I'm gone."

Sonia remembered her father's booming voice the last time Rafael had dared to suggest leaving for work. Felix had been enraged.

"You think Luis thought he would die this way? All of you young people think you know about the world, but you know nothing at all. Your good looks and hard work won't earn you the mercy of strangers. To the rest of the world, you're not anyone's son. You're just another hungry dog at their door."

Rafael read her mind as usual and encircled her in his arms.

"Papi is so dramatic. But he'll change his mind when our pockets are bulging and we can get him out of the mines."

Sonia shook her head. All she could imagine was her father staring at their empty beds. "It will kill him to have us both gone."

"I'm doing it *for* him, *hermanita.* Just like you, right?"

Sonia fell silent. The truth was that she was leaving to free herself of her burdens. Rafael, on the other hand, had been thinking of how best to bear them. She felt ashamed for all the times she'd envied his carefree ways. In his heart, he'd been figuring out how to be a man all along.

She leaned her head against his shoulder and sighed. "I want you to be safe."

"Pray to the wind, then," he teased.

"Stop it."

"I'll be *fine*. I've got everything worked out. Now, promise me your silence," he said, nudging her.

"I promise," she mumbled.

"That's a good sister. Oh! I almost forgot!" He reached into his shirt pocket and pulled out a delicate silver chain. "For you. So you can see I'm not cheap," he said, smiling.

Dangling on the end of the chain was a small charm in the shape of a large eye, the symbol for wisdom and clarity. The metal was thick and the workmanship flawless.

"It's beautiful, but look." She dumped her pouch of metal trinkets. "More and more *milagros*. Even without my shawl! I'm supposed to bless everyone while I'm gone. What a headache!"

He studied the pile and shrugged.

"Well, this one is just for you. My wish is for you to be happy." He fastened the necklace and walked her to the mirror. "The capital is a big place, *hermanita*, but you have a big heart and a big mind. Use them to find your path."

Sonia touched the pretty charm and held her brother tight.

A tiny scratching sound outside interrupted them. Rafael went to the window, just in time to see someone disappearing into the trees.

"*¿Quién vá?*"

But it was too late. The visitor was gone.

"Who could it have been?" Sonia asked.

"I don't know." Rafael picked up what had been left at the windowsill. "But they were looking for you."

A small note was addressed to her in the perfect penmanship of a scholar. Rafael read over her shoulder and pinched her devilishly as Sonia blushed under her smile.

"It looks as though I'm not the only one with midnight admirers," he said.

Good luck, Sonia, the note read. *Here is a new story to keep you company on the journey. I will miss you more than you know. If you ever need anything, you know where to find me.*

Here there were several erasures. Sonia read the closing carefully, imagining his handsome face, the feel of his hand in hers.

I will be thinking of you every day you are gone.
Pancho Muñoz

Chapter 7
Despedida

SONIA CLIMBED THE ladder of the passenger train in the fading afternoon light. Up close, it was a massive metal serpent, its blinding headlights glowing like eyes. Marco and his baggage clerk joked amiably as the other passengers boarded.

A seat had been reserved for her by a window, where she would have spectacular views of the mountains they would cross to reach the capital. She looked out at the crowd and searched the faces of the boys milling about at Señor Pasqual's taxi stand. She hoped Pancho would find the note she had dared to leave in his taxi's basket. Perhaps it had been a mistake to be so bold. She looked worriedly at the bored boys. What if one of them found what she had written first? What if the note somehow found its way to her father's hands?

Instinctively, she felt in her pocket for Pancho's story and for a small foil packet of her mother's cookies. She checked again under her seat to be sure she had not tipped the other food containers. Blanca had packed enough to eat for the long journey.

"Don't get off the train for anything," Tía Neli warned before kissing her niece on both cheeks. "Marco will leave you behind without a look back." She peered out the window and gazed far along the tracks. Rafael was not to be found at the train station.

"That brother of yours . . ." she muttered. "Whose arms is he in now?"

All around, the other passengers were talking and arranging their bags beneath their seats. Sonia sat back, grateful that she looked like any ordinary traveler. Her hair was pulled into a pretty braid along her back, and she wore a plain blue skirt and linen blouse, impeccably ironed by Blanca. Tía Neli had even looped small gold hoops through her ears. Best of all, her shawl was hanging back home in the kitchen.

She pulled out her traveling papers and reread the information carefully. Estación Punta Gorda would be their stop. She found it on Cuca's map. It was a tiny star outside the big swath that Cuca had marked clearly with an X.

At last Ramona, the most experienced of Señora

Masón's house staff, appeared. She carried a toddler on her hip as she made her way along the aisle. Though still a woman of only thirty, Ramona had been making this journey for at least a decade. Now she would leave behind her own son to serve as mother hen to three girls at Casa Masón. Sonia was to be her newest charge.

"Sonia!" she called down the aisle. "I almost didn't recognize you!"

Ramona's son, Manuel, squirmed, and she sat him in the empty seat beside Sonia. He looked disheveled, and sleep was still crusted in his eyes. As usual, he was clinging to his mother's skirts.

"Don't be nervous, Sonia," Ramona told her, sliding in beneath Manuel and bouncing him on her lap. "The ride is long but beautiful. We try to have fun and make the time go fast." She turned her son's face to Sonia. "Do you mind? A blessing? It would mean so much to his grandmother."

Sonia felt her smile harden as she placed her hand on Manuel's forehead and closed her eyes. She started to pray that he would not be lonely, but Manuel slapped her hand away before she was done. He scowled at his mother.

"*¿Dónde vás?*" he demanded angrily.

Ramona gave an apologetic look.

"Mami is going on an adventure again, Manuel. I am going to ride this big train over our mountains to see the

66

president's house. I'm going to the capital, where important people live."

"I want you to stay," he whined.

"But how will I have money to buy you things? You want me to buy you a new toy, don't you?"

Manuel leaned his head into her bosom and sucked his thumb.

"My mother babies him too much," she whispered over his head. Sonia nodded and held out a piece of her sugar cookie, but Manuel turned his head away and clutched his mother more tightly.

"Come along," Ramona told him, sighing. "Let's find your *abuela* outside. We can tell her what song to sing at bedtime tonight." She took Sonia's cookie and put it between her teeth before climbing down the steps.

Sonia watched them go. Manuel had not been fooled for a moment. He would miss his mother; no magic in the world would change that. His only option would be to learn to forget her a little bit each day until she was no more real than a photograph. Why hadn't she prayed for his courage to do that, instead?

Outside, Sonia's father stood smoking a Winston and guarding her bags as the workers tagged the pieces and tossed them inside the luggage compartment. Sonia felt too guilty to look into his face.

And Rafael was still nowhere to be found. That morning his bed was found unmade but empty. Their father, who was nursing his own headache from the party, had erupted like a boiling pot.

"Where is that boy? Doesn't he have any sense to know he has to see his sister off properly?" On and on he went until Blanca had begged him to calm himself.

"Rafael has always been a little sentimental, husband. He probably can't bring himself to see her go," she said.

Sonia felt a nervousness building inside her as her mother climbed aboard with last reminders.

"You remembered your money?"

"Yes."

"Your sweaters? The personal woman items? The *milagros* from the party? You can't forget those!"

Sonia held up a satchel, nearly bursting at the seams. Twice she had tried to leave it behind at the house, but Blanca kept finding it and placing it with her bags.

"*Sí, claro.* Everything."

Then her mother's eye fell on the sparkling charm at Sonia's neck. She held the unusual eye between her fingers.

"*Que bonito.* I haven't seen one that pretty in a long while."

"A going-away present from Rafael," Sonia explained, trying to sound casual.

"Rafael," Blanca said, shaking her head. "Where could he be? I can't find him anywhere, and your father is about to explode." She peered down the road for a sign of her son. "How could he let his own sister leave without saying good-bye?"

Sonia swallowed hard. She was beginning to hate herself for not having stopped him.

"You know Rafael, Mami," she said loyally. "He was out late last night—probably romancing someone. He's sleeping it all off, that's all."

Worry clouded her mother's face, and Sonia saw her mistake at once. Nothing plagued Blanca Ocampo more than her son's flirtations and the thought of where his transgressions with girls might lead. She had known more than one man in life who had died as the result of a jealous brawl.

"Scoundrel," she muttered. "He'll be sorry the moment he realizes he's missed you."

Sonia kissed her mother's hand to comfort her. "It's all right. Don't worry. Just tell him to start picking the color for his new truck."

Just then, Marco appeared at the top of the aisle.

"*¡Atención, señores!* All passengers take their seats. Tickets in your laps, please. Those who have no tickets must exit at once."

Her mother hugged her tightly. "Remember us, daughter. Never forget your mountain or your people."

Sonia watched her go. Then she pounded on the window until Felix turned at the vibrations and looked into her face. He tipped his hat and smiled with sad eyes.

The doors folded shut, and the train exhaled a burst of steam from its brakes. With a mournful whistle to announce their departure, the cars creaked into motion.

Ramona stared straight ahead as little Manuel held his ears and screamed. Sonia searched the faces of taxi boys until they all looked the same. Her parents waved and waved as the train gathered speed. She kept them in sight until they were specks in the distance, consumed in the yellow dust at the foot of their mountain.

CHAPTER 8
Felix and Tía Neli Wonder

IT WAS DIFFICULT to frighten a man like Felix Ocampo, Tía Neli mused. Darkness had never scared her brother. Blasts had not made him quiver. Not even the threat of being swallowed up in a crush of black earth had ever made him blink. He liked to brag that he was as hard and unyielding as the mountain itself.

But two days later, stooped in the garden over his tomatoes, Tía Neli could see that her brother was lost. He had stayed at the railway station long after Sonia's train disappeared and had then paced the kitchen floor, waiting for Rafael, who still had not appeared after all this time.

Finally, he'd sought refuge in the garden. He watched with disinterest as Tía Neli picked off the worms that were eating his vegetables.

"Fearing for one's children is far worse than any death," he told Tía Neli. "But they don't think about that, do they?"

"There's no use in becoming so melancholy," she scolded gently. "We will have word soon."

But he put his finger to his lips and pointed to his ear. *Listen.*

Tía Neli cocked her head and frowned. "You're hearing things again."

Felix Ocampo closed his eyes and concentrated stubbornly. "No, no. I am *not* hearing things. And that is exactly the problem. I should be hearing my children laugh and argue," he snapped. "This hush is burning my ears."

Tía Neli took off her apron and sat down beside him.

"Stop exaggerating," she said, biting into one of the few tomatoes that had survived the onslaught. But even as the words left her lips, she realized how quiet, indeed, the whole mountainside had been that day. Missing family left a space she had never imagined, especially with a new worry rising. She fingered the lace collar of her pretty dress and fell into somber thoughts of her own.

One problem solved, and another one on its heels. Where are you, Rafael?

"It's a bad omen, I tell you," Felix said, as if reading her mind. "Who knows what other troubles await us?" Rafael's name hung in the air unspoken.

Tía Neli gathered her sweater around her shoulders. She was a woman who prided herself on never letting life bully her, but now she felt unsure. She hated to admit it, but Felix was right: Who knew what lay ahead when children were cut free? They could become like loose kites on a windy day.

She helped Felix to his feet and walked him slowly inside the house, where Blanca was warming his tea. There was only one thing to do.

Seeking the path toward the plaza, Tía Neli set out to find some answers.

"He has been very busy today, *señora*, and it is nearly closing time," the secretary, Carmen, said firmly. "Come back again tomorrow."

Tía Neli considered the darkened sky, her swollen feet, and her tired back. She had been making inquiries about Rafael for hours, walking all over town until the heels of her shoes were worn to slants. She had already visited Capitán Fermín—useless as always; Juan, the barber; even the clerks at *los baratillos*, the shop where Rafael often bought cheap gifts for his endless stream of girlfriends. Señor

Arenas, with his greedy fingers on so many purses, might be just the man with answers.

"I'm afraid that's impossible. I know it's late, but it is urgent." She sat down and crossed her legs primly. "I'll wait."

Señor Arenas continued to shuffle papers as Tía Neli explained the delicate situation. When he had heard enough, he put up his hand.

"So what's the mystery here?" he said. "It sounds like your nephew has joined the parade north, *señora*. And if that's the case, what is it you think I can do for you? I run a legal operation here. I don't get mixed up in things that bring me headaches." He snapped shut a folder. "Carmen! Put away the files for the window factory!"

Tía Neli forced a polite smile while Carmen hurried about the room.

"Certainly, you are not a man of that underworld. No! It's just that the Ocampo family is most distressed. We thought an important man like you might hear things from time to time. Workers needed in far places who don't mind risk and are looking for a . . . less complicated way over?"

Carmen turned from the dented metal cabinet and lay down the file slowly. "*¿Algo más*, Carmen?" Señor Arenas said.

The secretary took her leave as Señor Arenas stood up and grabbed his hat from its hook.

"As I said: None of this concerns me. Now, with your permission, I'm afraid I am closed. I have an important meeting tonight that begins exactly now."

No doubt at the corner bar, Tía Neli mused.

"Of course. I'm sorry to have taken your time, *señor.* A thousand thanks. You are very kind."

Señor Arenas was already outside walking past his window by the time Tía Neli had bent to gather her purse.

"What are you doing there in the dark, brat?" she heard him shout. "Get your rusty contraption out of my way!"

Tía Neli crossed to the small window in time to see him give a young man an enormous pinch on the ear. When the boy looked up, she recognized him at once.

It was Pancho, the bike-taxi driver, caught eavesdropping at the window. His hair was uncombed, and he was out of breath. He stared at Tía Neli with his large eyes as he rubbed his ear.

"Well, you're certainly a rude one. My lovely niece, Sonia, will be very disappointed to know her school friend listens to other people's conversations," Tía Neli said through the window. "And look at the consequences! I have a good mind to pinch your other ear."

"Oh, please don't, *señora.* Forgive me! It is only that I

was told you were here in the plaza asking questions about Sonia's brother, and I thought it best—"

Tía Neli paused.

Why hadn't she thought of the taxi boy before? Every town had its eyes and ears—and always in the place one least expected it.

She hurried out to the street and examined Pancho's swollen ear. It was beginning to look like a pink cauliflower.

"Ice will fix that. We'll get some, and then, Pancho, you will tell me what you know."

"*A la orden, señora.* But remember I'm only a *taxista,*" he said, keeping his eyes down. "What can I know?" he asked.

Tía Neli patted his cheek. "Yes, you taxi boys are just as quiet as mice, but you're not stupid. Perhaps with a stop here or there, you'll think of the perfect someone who can tell me what I need to know."

He flashed her a quick smile and helped Tía Neli step aboard his cab. Soon Pancho was pedaling as hard as he ever had, moving like an arrow to its target.

Chapter 9
The Eyes and Ears of Tres Montes

¡Ay! THE TROUBLES of a taxi boy had no end.

Pancho tried to think of anything but the throbbing at the side of his head, which made him feel lopsided as he guided his bike taxi along the street. One day pompous men like Señor Arenas would think twice about taking such liberties with him, he mused darkly. The nerve of it made him want to punch out blindly. One day no one would call him Pancho. They would say, *Ah, Francisco Muñoz, of course, he's the famous poet from Tres Montes, the man who brings grown men to tears using only his pen! He is the president's favorite entertainer!* Never again would anyone say, *Pancho the Orphan, bike-taxi driver, whose ears you can yank like bread dough.*

He pedaled along the darkening streets, dodging dips and holes to keep Tía Neli comfortable. He had only been a full-time taxi boy for a few weeks, and while he was Señor Pasqual's favorite worker, he had found it was not an easy job at all. To be a good taxi boy, one had to live by absolute rules. You had to be stronger than a mule to haul fat passengers without grunting. You needed large eyes to see where you were going and sensitive ears to overhear the private conversations in case a passenger had plans to rob you. But the mouth? Mute, mute, mute. No secret overheard was ever to be shared.

"You're a taxi boy, not a parrot," is how Señor Pasqual put it.

Luckily, prudent silence came easily to people who were used to being insignificant. It was not hard at all for an orphan to be discreet with all he learned about people on his many rides. It was quite easy to ignore the names of lovers arranging clandestine meetings at midnight. Simple to forget picking up the drunken chief of police from a bar's doorstep. *Facilísimo* to close his ears to the many dark deals between men. He watched and listened and learned about surviving in the world, even in a tiny and seemingly simple place like Tres Montes.

In fact, he had only found it difficult to hold his tongue about two things in his entire life. One was his love for Sonia Ocampo, about whom he dreamed every night. Even awake, thoughts of her were distracting.

Why hadn't he kissed her when he had the chance? If he had, maybe she wouldn't be on a train going far away. Worse still, he had not come to see her off at the train station, and now, after discovering her letter, he was loathing himself. What if she never forgave him? Her letter filled his mind as he pedaled.

> *Pancho—*
>
> *I carry you in my heart to the capital. While I'm gone, take care not to listen to anyone who tells you what you can and can't be in life. It's a terrible fate, Pancho, one that both of us have to escape. If it's a poet you dream of becoming, then a poet you will be. Don't forget: You promised you would recite one of your poems for me.*
>
> *Until we are together under our tree again . . .*
>
> *Love from Sonia Ocampo*

Love, he thought. *Love from Sonia Ocampo.*

The words made his heart pound. What would he have said to her if he *had* gone to the train station?

For here was the second thing that he had ever found hard to keep from saying. It was a secret that would have clawed at his lips when he saw her. Alas, a taxi boy with large eyes and acute ears learns even the most dangerous plans of those he ferries here and there as they chase their dreams in the night.

And one of those young men had been none other than Rafael Ocampo.

CHAPTER 10
The Traitorous Conchita Fo

"Here?" Tía Neli looked around skeptically. "You want me to go in here? Alone? What kind of madman are you?"

Pancho had stopped in front of La Jalada, a dark establishment at the end of town. The stench of whiskey reached to where they stood on the street. Two sleeping drunks slumped like bookends on either side of the doorway.

"¿*Sola?* Not in a million years, *señora.*" He stepped off his bike and offered his elbow gallantly. "I will escort you."

"You'll tell me this instant why we're here," she said, unimpressed.

Pancho thought of the taxi-boy code of silence. Such a bother at times like this! "Do you mind if we at least get ice first, *señora?* In truth, my ear is killing me. Why, I can barely hear you!"

Tía Neli took his muscled arm and held her nose as she followed him inside.

Everyone knew that Conchita Fo, proprietor of La Jalada, had been fatally beautiful once. A singer in her youth, she had traveled to the capital and beyond, to cities far and wide in the North, enchanting men of every nation and leaving the resulting green-eyed children scattered along the way. She sold her deep voice for as long as she had been able to hold a tune. But time, drink, and a string of trouble with the law had left her with only La Jalada to her name—*that* and the distinction of knowing the secrets of more or less every man between Tres Montes and the capital. Even now, her figure could stir the longings of the many men who visited her establishment, including the taxi boys who came looking for fares or scraps of food. They could not help staring guiltily at her narrow waist, the seductive dip at the back of her neck. The plunge of her neckline made them wonder.

Conchita sat at the bar. She turned her shrewd eyes to Tía Neli and Pancho and let out a long plume of cigarette smoke in their direction.

"Look who's here, Mongo," she said to her tattooed barkeep. "Your favorite diversion."

The massive man looked up from the counter he was buffing and flashed a frightening smile. Mongo's teeth were all filed to sharp points, and a sleeve of tattooed flames rose along his arms and ended at his thick neck. He was frightful at first glance, but Pancho knew better. Mongo had once been an orphan himself, and all orphans knew about the loneliness of living like a parasite. So Mongo could be counted on for leftover snacks in exchange for one of Pancho's stories, especially if the tale involved knives — his passion.

"A new tale today, Pancho?" he asked. "Grab a stool."

"I'm afraid not this time, Mongo," Pancho replied. "Actually, *la señora* and I have come on important business."

Conchita Fo turned to them and regarded Tía Neli coldly. "Let me guess: You're looking for your man. Well, you can see he's not here, unless he's one of those two, in which case, you have my condolences." She pointed at the drunks. "If not, come back a little later. You can never tell who might turn up."

Tía Neli's mouth fell open, and her cheeks grew crimson.

"I happen to be a widow," she said. "And I can assure you, my husband wouldn't have ever come here. He was a decent man, who had the bad luck to be killed in a mine collapse. He never touched a drop of liquor in his life."

"What did you say your name is?" Conchita Fo asked.

83

"I didn't, but it's Neli Ocampo de Arroyo."

Conchita thought for a moment and smiled to show her perfectly white teeth.

"Of course. Guillermo Arroyo's woman," she said, as if they'd known each other all their lives. "We all miss him terribly."

"A million pardons, *señora*," Pancho said quickly before a clash of insults could dash his plan to pieces. "May I trouble someone for ice?"

Mongo stopped what he was doing and frowned. He gave Tía Neli a suspicious look as he popped two dirty ice cubes from a plastic tray.

"Next time, you break their nose first," he whispered, pressing them against the side of Pancho's head. "No matter who it is."

"Thanks, Mongo."

"It's my nephew we are here about," Tía Neli said. "Rafael Ocampo. Do you know him?"

Conchita Fo chuckled. "So. You are the family of that darling specimen? Lucky you to be a relation! Such a handsome young buck is hard to forget. Has he considered being in the cinema?"

Tía Neli straightened her shoulders. "Have you any idea where he might be? We are crazy with worry trying to locate him."

"*¿Quién yo?*" Conchita looked with feigned surprise at Mongo. "She acts as though men tell me their secrets!"

"Arenas suggested that Rafael has gone north," Tía Neli persisted. "Do you know if it's true?"

"*El norte.* Everyone loves the idea." Conchita sighed. "I spent years there entertaining my faithful public and for what? It is as brutal a place as any, *señora*, for those of us cursed with humble beginnings. Look at me. Right back where I started."

"Well, taking a risk might be better than starving," Tía Neli said.

Conchita took a long drag of her cigarette. "Some would say that, *señora*. Of course, those of us who stay behind aren't the ones who are bending our backs to work, are we? We are—what do we call it?—the beneficiaries of their sacrifice." Her eyes traveled along the fancy lace of Tía Neli's collar.

Pancho could hear Tía Neli's teeth grinding. He scrambled between them just in time.

"Excuse me for speaking," he said. "But look! I have found something here on the floor, *señora*. I'm very sure it's yours."

He smiled and pressed the only bill he had earned that day into Conchita Fo's hand. "Forgive me for interrupting. Go on. You were about to tell *la señora* about her nephew."

Conchita let out six perfect smoke rings and stubbed out her cigarette as they floated through the air. Pancho watched Mongo carefully; he was buffing the same spot a bit too ferociously.

"I heard some men talking about a trip," Conchita said with a shrug. "He might have been among them. I can't recall exactly."

Tía Neli planted her feet. "Who were those men?" she whispered, leaning in.

"Now, how would my customers like it if their secrets were shared with anyone who came asking? Don't put me in such a position, *señora*. It's bad business."

Tía Neli's face was mere inches from Conchita Fo's. "The men's names, *por favor*." It sounded like a threat.

"Heavens, *señora*!" Pancho interrupted again. "I almost forgot!" He held up his lucky silver piece and placed it on the bar, without a second thought about how he would miss its comforting weight in his pocket. "To your continued beauty and good fortune!"

Conchita patted Pancho's face sweetly and tucked the coin in her bosom with a flourish. "All I can tell you is this," she said, turning to Tía Neli once again. "He left here with a man who barely knows what he's doing. These are dangerous times for an inexperienced man to bring boys across, *señora*. Anything can happen crossing the Haunted Valley—you know that. That's how we get dead boys tossed out on the road." She signed the cross over herself.

"Pancho!"

The sharp voice echoed inside the empty bar. At the door was the silhouette of Armando, a younger *taxista*. He was perspiring and panting.

"I've been crazy looking for you! Good thing I saw your bike outside."

"What is it, then?" Pancho asked, racing for the door.

Armando stared at the swollen mass at the side of Pancho's head. "What's wrong with your ear?"

"Never mind that!"

Armando shrugged and pointed at the dirty clock over the door. "Señor Pasqual needs you at the mayor's house in thirty minutes, hands and feet washed. There's a party."

"Forgive me, *señora*," Pancho told Tía Neli. "I must go at once. May I take you home?"

By the time Tía Neli arrived at her door, her face was crumpled with grief.

"Stay calm, *señora*," Pancho told her. "You never know what is coming around the bend. Perhaps a solution lies up ahead on our path."

Tía Neli shook her head sadly. "Go on, Pancho. You'll be late, and you shouldn't keep the mayor waiting. This is in the hands of God now."

Moments later he was careening down the mountain, his mind whirling as fast as his wheels.

In God's hands? Or would a taxi boy's hands have to do?

CHAPTER 11

Crossing the Haunted Valley

THE WORLD BEYOND Tres Montes was glorious. How irritating that her parents had tried to keep her—and Rafael—from it. Sonia pressed her nose to the train window, wishing that her brother were by her side to enjoy the view.

The train had climbed high along rickety tracks and then lumbered into La Fuente, the place the Gypsies called the Haunted Valley. It was a long and deserted stretch between mountain peaks that belched plumes of smoke. No Gypsy ever crossed La Fuente; they claimed it was filled with the restless spirits of all who died there.

They lurched around perilous turns that opened unexpectedly to dizzying canyon views. Hawks hung outside her window, and far below there were waterfalls cascading into rushing rivers, where rainbows rose in the mist, like bridges to some other world. It seemed like an eternity before they found civilization again, stopping at last in a town that was even smaller than Tres Montes. Mule-drawn carts waited, laden with stews and meat pies for sale along the tracks. Passengers in other cars got out to stretch their legs, but Sonia, remembering Tía Neli's advice, hung out the window to get air. Soon hands were reaching up. Children, a woman with no teeth, even a young man about Rafael's age, who walked stooped and with a cane.

"He must have come through the valley," Eva whispered to her, when she saw Sonia staring at the beggar. "One of the lucky ones."

Sonia, still too nervous to eat, tossed him down all that her mother had packed.

Silence descended on the train that night as it chugged through yet another pine forest, dark as a wolf's mouth. The other passengers were sleeping uncomfortably in their seats. Even Marco, who had been making eyes at her all day, had grown pensive and was now far off at the front of the locomotive. Ramona was snoring softly, too.

Sonia settled in once again to read Pancho's story. She was grateful for the distraction and had savored it slowly throughout the long ride. The adventure kept her from thoughts of Rafael, which seemed to find her even more frequently after seeing the beggar. Instead of worrying, she could lose herself in Pancho's world of a beautiful Arabian girl born mute and kept prisoner by her silence and her warlord uncle. She thought of Pancho's intelligent eyes and the long fingers with which he would have turned each page if they were reading under their shade tree. Would he really be thinking of her every day? She hoped so. If only he could know the truth about why she had left, without hating her for being a fraud, Sonia thought. If only Pancho knew she was trapped in silence, just like the girl in his story.

Footsteps stopped near her seat.

"Hungry?" Eva held out a napkin with white cheese and crackers she'd bought at the last station.

Sonia reached politely for a morsel. "Thank you."

She was already fond of Eva, who had pointed out sights on the trip all afternoon and made the time go by with explanations of what girls were wearing in the capital, what colors most favored her skin, whose boyfriend was running around with whom. She was a fount of personal information about others, but she seemed without malice. Best of all, she treated Sonia as if they'd been friends for years.

"The first time in the city is always exciting, isn't it, *amor*?"

Sonia nodded. "Don't tell me it ever gets boring!"

"*¡Ay, no!* Just being rid of that dull beast Irina Gomez makes it exciting. Do you know she had the nerve to tell my mother that nail enamel is for harlots?" She held up her newly manicured hands as proof of the impossible. "Such a killjoy!"

Sonia shook her head and turned back to the window, thinking of Pancho once again. "Irina Gomez knows nothing," she agreed.

"What are you reading?" Eva asked, peering at the story.

Sonia folded it quickly.

"Nothing important," she said, stuffing Pancho's gift in her bag.

"A private person, I see," Eva observed coyly. "I like a girl with secrets. Anyway, *corazón*, the important thing is we're free. We're practically women now, off to work—and not the kind of jobs that pay pennies, the way they do at home. We're going to earn real money—more than a country schoolmistress, for certain. That's probably why Irina Gomez hates us."

Suddenly the train whistle blew, and the wheels screeched to a halt. Eva was thrown against the seat ahead of her. Sonia's satchel of *milagros* clattered as it fell to the floor and rolled away.

"Why are we stopping?" Sonia tried to sound calm. She

thought of train robbers and bandits. There were no station lampposts in sight. Outside, only blackness.

"God deliver us if it's a boulder from a landslide." Eva rubbed the bump on her head and sucked her teeth irritably. "Last year we were stuck in this valley for five hours."

Ramona, deep in sleep, did not stir. Eva peered out into the night and then called to someone farther back in the train car.

"*Mi amor,*" she whispered. "Go sweet-talk Marco. Find out what's going on."

Dalia made her way up the aisle. Her curly brown hair wasn't bouncing loose around her face, as it had been at the party. Instead, it was tucked behind her ears demurely. Unlike Eva, she hadn't spoken a word to Sonia. In fact, she showed no interest in her—or in anyone else, for that matter.

"That fool probably fell asleep at the switch," Dalia said. She ignored the NO ADMITTANCE sign and slid back the door to the locomotive. In a moment their voices were murmurs. Laughter floated through the cars.

Sonia watched with fascination, thinking of something her mother often said. *"In the arms of a beautiful woman, a man's mouth runs like a river."*

What might her besotted brother confess to a pretty girlfriend? Maybe he had shared the specifics of his plans.

"Stupid cows on the tracks," Dalia announced when she returned a little while later.

"Oh, well, that's not too bad," Eva said, turning to Sonia.

But Sonia wasn't thinking about cows as she watched Dalia recede into the darkness. She started down the aisle.

"Where are you going?" Eva asked.

"The facilities." She held her stomach as if it were cramped.

"The toilet hasn't worked for the last three hours," Eva said. "Prepare yourself, *corazón*. It's a horror."

Sonia hurried off, searching the dark seats for Dalia's shape. She found her at last, sitting alone at the back and staring out at the sky. For a moment neither girl spoke.

"You look like him." Dalia was studying her in the reflection of the darkened window. "The eyes, I think."

"Thank you."

Sonia crouched low in the aisle and whispered, "Dalia, do you know where Rafael is?"

Turning, Dalia regarded her with a cold look.

"What Rafael tells his friends is his own business, Sonia. Take it from me," she said with an ugly smirk. "If there's one thing he appreciates, it's a girl who can keep her mouth shut about what he's up to."

"But he must have told you he was leaving. I'm his

blood, Dalia; I have the right to know." She looked around at the sleeping passengers to make sure she was not being heard. "What if evil finds him?"

"*Por Dios*, let your brother do what he has to do. He knows his risks."

"Please," Sonia continued. "I'm worried."

"Worry about something else, then—like your own hide. Or didn't your bossy aunt tell you that you'll have plenty to keep you busy at the widow's house?"

Loyalty fueled Sonia's growing temper. "Take care how you speak of my aunt. She's done me a great favor. I owe Tía Neli nothing but thanks."

"Thanks?" Dalia clicked her tongue and shook her head as though Sonia were someone to be pitied. "Go sit down, *niña*." The train started to move. "Rafael would never forgive me if his precious little sister got hurt on the journey." With that, she turned back to the window.

Sonia found her empty seat. Anger was stuck in her throat like a lump of bread. The thought of working with a girl so hateful made her want to scream.

"Are you sick, *amor*?" Eva asked. "You don't look well." She gasped and sniffed the empty napkin in her lap. "Did I poison you with rancid food?"

Sonia shook her head and curled up in her seat. She called to her grandmother in her mind, but the only sound was the train inching forward and the terrible protest of cows against someone's leather switch. She moved as close as she dared to Ramona and thought of her brother.

"What are you humming?" Ramona said, a little while later. "It sounds so sad."

"Me? Nothing." Sonia hadn't even realized she was making a sound. "Just an old miners' tune."

CHAPTER 12
La Capital

SONIA AWOKE AND rubbed the last threads of awful dreams from her eyes. Rafael had been drowning in the river, calling her name as the current dragged him to the froth near the waterfall like the ones in La Fuente. *Sonia,* he called. But no matter how hard she paddled toward him, he was always just out of reach in the mist.

When she sat up, heart still pounding, she stared out the window in awe.

The golden dome of the presidential palace shimmered opulently against the dawn sky. They had reached the capital at last, and now she could see that it was even more magnificent than she had ever imagined. The old cliff-side city had withstood the centuries proudly, its grandeur untouched by modern vulgarities, like highways or architecture in glass or chrome. Here the roads were still cobblestone, and the buildings were preserved like European palaces. Potted bougainvillea climbed up columns to the wrought-iron balconies that overlooked the main thoroughfare. Shop doors were inlaid with stained glass. Even the railway station was a work of art. Its intricate mosaic floors were befitting of a sultan's quarters.

As the train came to a stop, Ramona walked the aisle to shake her charges awake. She snapped her fingers in front of Sonia's unblinking eyes.

"Gather your things," she said. "We're here."

It took six breezy trolley stops and a fifteen-minute walk along the rows of trumpet trees to arrive at Casa Masón from the railway. But when they at last crossed the gates of the estate, Sonia could scarcely believe her eyes. There were fountains with stone nymphs, exotic flowers, and two aloof greyhounds lounging elegantly on a carpet of grass. Several other large homes peeked over hedges nearby. Punta Gorda was clearly the most luxurious neighborhood in the capital.

Sonia took care to stay beside Eva, who chatted as though she were a tour guide.

"It's very ordinary," Eva said importantly, "to see famous people sunning themselves on a patio, so be sure not to gawk. Last year I even saw the president's wife exercising her mare in *la señora*'s paddock." She lowered her voice. "She's a graceless rider. No posture at all. A rancher could do better."

"The president's wife?" Sonia exclaimed. She would write to Pancho at once to tell him.

Ramona led them along the fieldstone path until it cleaved in two. She straightened her wrinkled skirt and turned to hand Eva a key.

"Air out our quarters." She motioned to the path that wound around the back of the house. "Dalia will wait here for the luggage cart; it's on its way. I'll let them know we've arrived."

After the long peal of the doorbell quieted, Sonia craned her neck to see who opened the door. It was an old woman, nearly bent in two with age, with an unpleasant face to match her crooked body. She motioned for Ramona to step inside.

"*That's* Señora Masón?" she asked.

"Certainly not!" Eva said. "That's only Teresa. She runs everything around here."

"But she's so old," Sonia blurted out.

"And unfortunately still alive," Dalia muttered.

Seeing Sonia's astonishment, Eva shook her head. "Dalia's right. You'll have to keep your eye on that *vieja*. Teresa is *la señora*'s best spy."

With that, Eva started down the second path. "Well? Are you coming?"

The greyhounds dashed past the girls in a blur. It felt good to move after so many hours on a train, especially in a yard of such splendor. The interior garden was magnificent. How her father would love such a place! Bottlebrush trees were heavy with an army of thirsty monarch butterflies; a stone bridge arched over a fishpond carpeted with lily pads; roses of every variety perfumed the air. Around the first bend were the horse stables, and then came a large garage, where bored drivers were buffing long black cars. The young men stopped to wave as the girls passed. Eva pushed out her bosom a little farther.

They walked on, arm in arm, as though in a park, until all that was left of the main house was the tile rooftop over the trees.

"What is Señora Masón like?" Sonia asked. "She must be so elegant to live in a grand place like this."

"Elegant, yes. Friendly, never," Eva explained. "But I suppose that's natural. She learned long ago not to love servants, *mi vida.*"

According to Eva, who had read the story in the old society pages, one of the biggest scandals of the day was the death of Katarina Masón's nanny. The family dog had bitten the *manejadora de niños* savagely on the ankle.

"Imagine it! The nanny survived twenty-nine of her scheduled thirty-one injections before dying rabid—screaming in terror at the sound of running water." She lowered her voice. "I'll bet it took a downpour of money to quiet that girl's family."

Sonia looked around cautiously for the greyhounds, but just then Eva stopped and pointed at a charming house up ahead. It overlooked neatly trimmed grass and benches. Flowers of every kind draped opulently from window boxes on the second floor.

"There. Your new home, *mi amor*. We call it La Casita."

Sonia stood dumbfounded. "For us? *This?*" Back home it could have been the mayor's house.

"I told you it was marvelous. Come inside." They ran toward it.

The doorknob on the carved front door was shiny brass. Eva let Sonia unlock the door and led her inside to the sitting room, where they stood in silence for moment, staring. The space was dark and musty, and the furniture was still covered in sheets.

"It's always a bit of a cave at first." Eva opened the thick drapes and cranked open the front shutters. "It will feel like home soon enough, *mi amor*. Here."

She balled the sheets under her arm and tossed them to Sonia before heading toward the stairs, which she climbed two at a time. Sonia let her fingers trail along the pretty wood of the handrail as she followed in awe. On the landing below, the dogs dashed madly in happy circles, barking and upending a chair with their muscular legs.

"Here they are!" Eva called from somewhere ahead.

Sonia followed her friend's voice down the hall to the last bedroom, where she found her digging inside a claw-footed wardrobe in the corner. In a moment Eva emerged, red-faced and triumphant.

"This is my favorite part of the capital!" She dragged out a box of old books and reached inside. Spiderwebs clung to the binding of the volume she pulled out.

"Books?" Sonia didn't remember Eva ever being studious for Irina Gomez.

"Not just books! Timeless stories of love!" Eva pressed her lips to the curly gold script on the cover. "Thank God they're safe."

They were old romances. Sonia thought that none of those stories could possibly compare to Pancho's inventions, but she kept her lips sealed on the matter, remembering the shame of her classmates' teasing. Instead, she looked around carefully at her new room. The plaster walls of their bedroom were cracked in several places, but otherwise the room was pleasant—clean and simple, with two small beds, a wardrobe, and nightstand. The next room was more or less a duplicate, except for the view. From the arched window between Sonia's and Eva's beds, one had a sweeping vista of the grounds.

She stepped out to the balcony and took in a deep breath of winter jasmine. Sonia felt like the victorious girl in Pancho's story, the one who had brandished a golden sword, slayed her uncle, and fled from her captors on horseback.

"Of course, you've taken the best room for yourselves."

The cold voice made Sonia turn. Dalia was standing at the bedroom door with Sonia's suitcases.

"I will have to resign myself to the room right across the hall, I suppose," she continued.

Sonia, still bruised from their encounter on the train, did not reply.

Dalia was not fazed in the least.

"Here." She tossed a set of keys roughly at Sonia. "Don't lose them."

Sonia studied the keys curiously. At home no one used more than an eye hook to hold a door shut. Looking now, Sonia noticed dead bolts on each of the bedroom doors.

"Locks? Even on the inside of the house?" She turned to Eva. "Are there bandits here?"

But Eva was already languishing in bed, entranced by the first pages of her favorite saga. It was Dalia who replied.

"Lesson one: There are criminals everywhere, Sonia." She smiled wryly. "Sometimes we can barely trust our own housemates."

CHAPTER 13
Servants

SONIA WAS SURE it was Rafael pulling on her braid when she opened her eyes in the darkness. Her whole life she had been awakened by his nonsense, followed by the piercing crows of their neighbor's rooster and her mother bringing cinnamon milk to her in bed.

"Stop it or I'll bite you, I swear it!" she muttered as she dug inside her covers.

It took a moment to realize it wasn't her brother at all.

"*Despierta, mi amor.* We'll be late."

Eva, her hair set in pin curls, was leaning over her.

Sonia sat up groggily; the trip had exhausted her more than she'd realized. The first light of dawn was glowing through the slats in the shutters.

Eva buzzed around the room to get ready. One hand yanked her curls loose as she tried to unfasten the stubborn buttons of her uniform with the other. She slipped the shapeless black sheath over her head, and the curves and slopes of her youth disappeared.

"Yours is in the wardrobe," she said, wrinkling her nose as she studied her reflection. "Don't worry about the size. Nothing helps. You'll look just as dreadful as the rest of us. Open the shutters, *cariño.*"

Outside, the ground staff was already busy. Stable boys carried hay, and the old gardener was watering roses. The milkman was making his delivery at the back gate. Sonia spied Ramona and Dalia crossing the wet grass toward the main house, too. From here, they looked like old crows, identical in their black uniforms, opaque stockings, and square-toed shoes. It was a world away from the lively colors of Tres Montes and the friendly cries from doorways wherever you went. *¡Buenos días! ¿Qué tal? ¿Qué se cuenta?*

"*¡Apúrate pues!*" urged Eva again. "Hurry! This is no way to make a first impression!"

Sonia dressed in a flash and giggled with Eva at their dowdy appearance. She paused at the wardrobe before she left, contemplating the satchel of *milagros.*

Soon they were hurrying to follow the flock, the jangling of metal trinkets in Sonia's pocket marking each step.

Though she would always hate to admit it, Sonia put Rafael and all her other regrets out of her mind for the rest of that day. She did not let herself think about her brother somewhere on his reckless journey. She ignored the memory of her father's sighs and of the chivalrous look in Pancho's eyes. Instead, she lost herself in the world of a proper household apprentice.

She scurried from room to room, pulling up her baggy stockings and trying to memorize Ramona's endless instructions about how to make a household run with the precision of a navy ship. It took no time to realize that there were domestic arts in existence that no one in Tres Montes would have ever imagined necessary. Here one used an ostrich-plume duster instead of an old shirt to clean the teardrop chandeliers that shone like diamonds. Sugar was served in silver containers, which had to be polished wearing gloves. Her shoulders grew numb from rubbing them clean.

"When will I know I'm done?" Sonia asked, holding one up to the light.

Ramona laughed. "When you can count your eyelashes in the reflection, of course."

The dining room proved the most confusing in the end. Sonia had never given thought to rules about setting a table. At home, she laid out a plate for each person, fork and knife on either side. But again, the rules here were completely different—and unbendable.

Eva was her tutor. She gave Sonia a pair of white cotton gloves and clicked open a carved chest. Sonia gasped when Eva revealed the silverware.

"All this for a single meal?" Sonia asked. "Do they use a different fork for each bite?"

Eva giggled. "Pay attention, *mi vida*. There's a lot to know."

Forks on the left, knives and spoons to the right, but with the cutting edge facing *in*. There were tiny forks for oysters and little knives just for butter. And if dessert was to be served, the forks and spoons were to be placed above the plate or bowl.

"Not that one," Eva told her, surveying her first attempt. "The short one is for salad." She pursed her lips and moved the water glass to its proper place. Sonia had placed it where the wine glass belonged. "Let's try again."

"How long are you going to be at this?" The girls turned to find Teresa glaring. "Is the girl a dunce?"

The old woman had materialized from nowhere. She glanced down disapprovingly at Sonia's droopy stockings.

"We were just finishing, Teresa," Eva mumbled. "Sonia is a fast learner."

Teresa snorted.

"We'll see. What can we expect from mountain girls who eat with their fingers, for God's sake."

Sonia felt herself go tense as Teresa hobbled over to inspect the table setting. She adjusted the silverware closer to the table's edge with the expression of a woman accustomed to the worst.

"The parlor is thick with dust," she said. "Go."

Sonia nodded and hurried for the door, only too happy to escape.

"Where are you going, you silly girl!" Teresa snapped. "It's *that* way."

"Ignore her," Eva whispered later as they rinsed out their stockings and got ready for bed. "She's been stuck here as a domestic since she was a girl. She makes everyone suffer with her."

Sonia's neck and shoulders were aching. Teresa had

made her dust the parlor twice. "But it can't be *that* sad living in a place like this," she protested.

Eva climbed into bed and reached under her pillow with a devilish look. "Let's forget about Teresa, all right? Close your eyes, *mi vida*. I'll treat you to a scandalous bedtime story."

Sonia was fast asleep by the third page.

CHAPTER 14
Breakfast Service

"SHOW ME YOUR fingernails."

Ramona inspected Sonia carefully and nodded her approval. It would be the first day for Sonia to serve Katarina Masón in person, and no detail was to be missed.

"First impressions are everything," she said, just the way Tía Neli would have.

Sonia looked nervously at Dalia, whom Ramona had selected as her mentor for the breakfast service. What could be worse? Dalia had already complained loudly about having to look after Sonia's work.

"It's either serve breakfast or stay here and boil the feathers off those chickens I put in the ice chest for you," Ramona had said evenly. She was the only one who could stomach the stench of wet carcasses without retching.

"Fine." She thrust a silver tray at Sonia. "Keep your eyes open and your mouth shut."

Ramona placed a full coffeepot on the tray and took Sonia's face in her hands. "Don't be nervous. If you forget what I've taught you, watch how Dalia serves; she's an angry wasp in the kitchen, but she's excellent at serving, the very best we have." She paused to think of last-minute warnings. "Remember: speak only when asked a direct question, and reply—"

"In your softest tone and with the fewest words possible," Eva added in a startling singsong voice. It was as if the ghost of Irina Gomez had put the words on her lips. She smiled at Sonia mischievously and returned to arranging the pastries. Sonia bit her lip to avoid laughing.

"If you know so much, Eva, why have you prepared this tray so poorly?" Ramona asked.

"Poorly? What do you mean?" Eva looked at Sonia's tray. "*Café, tostadas con miel,* a poached egg, and two pastries." She crossed her arms primly. "What have I forgotten?"

Ramona rolled her eyes to the heavens. "Señora is hosting her nephew this morning. We'll need another cup and saucer. Show Sonia where to get them."

Eva's face dropped. "Señor Umberto is here?"

"I hate it when you girls are not observant. He arrived last night. Why else would I have ordered raspberry *pasteles*? They're all that young man will eat!" Ramona exclaimed.

Eva exchanged a careful glance with Dalia as she led Sonia into the dining room, where the French cabinet was filled with breakfast ceramics. She pulled a blue cup from a hook.

"You'll have to be extra careful, *mi vida*," Eva whispered when they were both hidden behind the large doors.

"Careful with what?"

"Shhh! With Señor Umberto, of course! He's gorgeous, but—"

Ramona poked her head through the swinging door, and Eva fell silent. The grandfather clock began chiming the hour.

"Hurry, girls!" Ramona said. "She's not to be kept waiting."

Eva gave Sonia an apologetic look.

"Come on," Dalia called over her shoulder as she swept past them toward the stairs. "Or do I have to do this myself?"

The sound of Sonia's thick heels clicked in time with Dalia's as they made their way along the marble hallway to the bedrooms. Sonia grew more frightened with each step. This was her first time in the upstairs chambers—Señora Masón's most private area of the house. And it was the first time she would lay eyes on her employer. She had seen Señora Masón only from a distance. The many portraits around the house showed a proud silver-haired woman with no smile.

By the time they reached the door, her hands were shaking so violently that the coffee was in a puddle.

Dalia looked at the mess in disgust. There was no time to return to the kitchen, so she untied the ends of her apron and mopped the tray. Then she stuffed the dirty apron behind a potted palm. "I won't help you again, so calm yourself. And while you're at it, get that look off your face. You're not going to an execution."

With that, she opened the double doors and stepped inside.

That Katarina Masón was already waiting—impeccably powdered, dressed, and combed—did not surprise Sonia. Eva had already told her that the woman was a well-known insomniac and had been since the night her husband, Don Carlos Masón, died without warning in their bed while eating red grapes and cheese. According to the gossip columns, he'd been a sweet buffoon—but one with blood cold enough for running a business and living with a spoiled woman. From the day he left her a widow, she awoke at four o'clock each morning to read all the society pages in the capital. Then she personally arranged her grueling social calendar, a task she trusted to no secretary. Eva claimed that she spent her time trading stories with the wives of government officials and gambling away her husband's endless fortune on horse races.

"Muy buenos días, Señora Masón," Dalia said.

Teresa, who handled the most intimate details of Katarina Masón's elaborate toilette, looked up from folding a silk nightdress. When she saw the two girls, her face soured.

"You're late," she muttered. "We run a disciplined house, *oyeron?"*

Sonia crossed the room to set down the tray, in the exact manner as Dalia. She was within inches of Katarina Masón and could smell her perfume. She was a woman in her fifties, but with the unmistakable air of the rich and well cared for, she looked only a few years older than Ramona. Already in pearls, she sat across from a young man who wore a white linen suit and had topaz rings on his fingers. The young man had the same piercing blue eyes as his aunt, the same air of the upper class. He could have been a school chum of Rafael's if they'd been born in the same circles, Sonia thought, studying him from the corner of her eye. Eva was right. He was handsome. Still, his good looks instantly made her more nervous.

"Hello," Umberto said, showing off a bright smile.

Sonia nodded and looked down at once.

He smiled pleasantly as he watched Dalia unload the things on her tray. When one of the dogs snapped at the pastries, he reached protectively for her hand.

"You'd better be careful! These beasts have a mind of their own. They'll bite your pretty fingers off like tasty sausages." He lowered his voice and winked. "I can't say I'd blame them."

Dalia took back her hand and set the silverware without hesitation. "I'm not afraid of dogs, *señor.*"

Señora Masón opened the morning paper and squinted. "I need light," she said briskly.

It took Teresa's piercing glare for Sonia to realize that Señora Masón was talking to her.

Sonia pulled back the brocade curtains and cranked open the windows. The morning sunshine streamed in from the balcony and warmed the whole room in a pretty glow that gave Sonia pause. Finches darted in the potted hibiscus as she tied back the sashes. The sight of them made her remember Pancho, who sometimes clipped blooms and left them anonymously on her chair at school. She was still in her daydream when she turned back to see Umberto smiling wolfishly at her.

"And who is this little lovely thing, Tía?" he said to his aunt. "You haven't introduced us."

Sonia blushed.

Teresa turned from the bureau, where she was arranging lace handkerchiefs, and looked from Sonia to Umberto. Then she frowned.

"Tell Señor Umberto your name," she ordered. "They do teach manners in the countryside, don't they?"

Sonia felt her mouth go dry as everyone waited. "Sonia Ocampo, *señor*. It's a pleasure to meet you."

"The pleasure is all mine," he said. "I hope you're enjoying your work here so far."

Katarina Masón put down her paper and regarded Sonia carefully. "How old are you?" she asked.

"Sixteen, *señora*."

She shook her head and picked up her paper.

"What is Arenas sending me, Teresa?" she asked. "This one still has her milk teeth! I'll have to complain. Remind me."

Sonia stared at her shoes.

"Tía," Umberto exclaimed. "I think that's too harsh.

117

Sixteen is a perfect age to leave the nest. She's young and pretty, that's all." He smiled at Sonia in a way that made her feel worse. Then he motioned to the selection of pastries on the tray.

"What do you recommend?"

Before Sonia could reply, Dalia plucked a raspberry tart from the bunch and dropped it on his plate. If he'd been a boy at home, Sonia was sure Dalia would have plucked his eyes out instead.

"Fill the cups," Dalia ordered.

Umberto leaned back, chomping on the *pastel* as Sonia poured the coffee. The corners of his mouth were soon stained red with jam. He was looking devilishly from Sonia to Dalia, openly comparing the merits of their waists and hips, when the sunlight from the balcony made Sonia's necklace glitter like a star.

"Come here." He motioned to Sonia.

For a long moment, she did not move. A boy had never ordered her about, not even Rafael. She looked to Dalia for help, but her expression was blank.

Teresa, however, seemed angrier by the moment. "Did you hear what Señor Umberto said? He's called you. Go."

Sonia set down the pot and went to him. Umberto took the eye charm between his sticky fingers and flashed a smile as he pulled her a little closer. His breath was on her shoulders, and his eyes flitted over her bosom.

"Where did you get such a necklace, Sonia Ocampo?" he cooed. "It must have cost a pretty penny." He looked at his aunt, whose jewelry collection was the talk of every woman in the capital. "What do you think, Tía?"

Señora Masón laid down her paper again and looked over the top of her reading glasses irritably.

"What a question, nephew! Next you'll confuse glass with sapphire. It's a cheap rural piece, of course, from the interior," she said. "The countryside is full of those *milagros* — and the little superstitions that go with them."

Sonia forced herself not to speak. *Milagros* were pounded with care into the shape of each person's hope, she knew. They weren't cheap — in any way.

"But where did you get it?" Umberto insisted, holding his nose rudely to the metal and helping himself to another look inside her uniform.

She tugged firmly enough to step back.

"It was a going-away gift," she said quietly.

"Oh," he said, pouting. "A boyfriend, I suppose."

Suddenly, he screamed and jumped back from the table. Hot coffee was steaming in his lap and dripping onto the Oriental rug.

"You stupid girl!" he shouted at Dalia. "You've ruined my suit! I'm scalded!"

"A million pardons," Dalia said without a trace of remorse in her voice. She looked at Sonia severely. "We will need more coffee. Fetch it now."

Old Teresa snatched the coffeepot from Dalia, complaining loudly about the shabby qualifications of modern workers.

"You'll do well to call Arenas, *señora*," Teresa said.

Sonia backed from the room, her eyes meeting Dalia's for a split second as the insults rained down. She'd scalded him on purpose; Sonia was sure of it. Dalia was never careless.

She raced all the way to the kitchen, grateful that Ramona was at the gate, arguing with the grocer about a bill. How would she explain such a catastrophe?

Eva shook her head as she filled a new carafe, listening to Sonia's account of what happened.

"Hmpf." She buttoned up her uniform to the chin and pushed the door open with her bottom. "Stay here, *mi vida*."

Sonia watched her disappear through the door. The kitchen suddenly felt empty and large. Teresa would have Ramona's ear about Dalia before the day was through.

Sonia sat down at the worktable, her mind carefully

going over the morning's events. What could she do to repair them? She knew all the girls would pay for what happened—even Dalia.

She changed into her work apron, her hands still shaking. The birds in the ice chest were all plucked and chilled by the time the others returned.

CHAPTER 15
Market Day for an Exemplary Apprentice

"WHO EVER HEARD of such a thing? Two girls needed to buy the bread and cheeses in town? *¡Qué cosa!* People will say we're hiring the simpleminded!" Old Teresa grimaced at the sprig of daisies she was arranging in a vase.

"I want them to go," Dalia said from the corner, where she was carving radishes into rosebuds. "I'll finally get my work done in peace."

"And who asked your opinion?" Teresa barked.

"I think it's the perfect day for the girls to go," Ramona said. "*La señora* will be at the polo matches today. Have you forgotten? We won't have guests to worry about. Besides, Sonia hasn't seen the city yet."

"That one?" The old woman rolled her eyes to the heavens. "She needs to learn hard work, that's all. She won't learn that by strolling around like an empress!"

Ramona smiled at Teresa. "I've heard Oscar say *you* were once quite a beauty strolling along the avenues, too."

Sonia tried not to gape at the thought. It was impossible to imagine a shriveled crone like Teresa being carefree and pretty.

"Keep this in a safe place, *oíste*?" Ramona handed Eva several bills.

"No one will lay his hands on this," Eva promised, tucking it inside her brassiere.

"Unless you want him to," Dalia muttered.

"And for you, the list," Ramona told Sonia. "Don't forget: It's the stop by the amphitheater. The stop after *that* is Colonia Vásquez." She shuddered and pointed at Sonia's shiny charm. "Tuck that in. Pickpockets and thieves are the order of the day there."

Eva hooked a basket over her wrist and pointed to the kitchen clock, her eyes shiny with excitement.

"Let's go, *cariño*!" She grabbed Sonia by the elbow and hurried toward the door. "We'll miss the morning trolley!"

Using Cuca's map, they got off at the appointed stop and climbed the steep hills toward the market. Unlike Tres Montes, the shops here were all indoors and boasted elegant plate-glass windows. Eva dallied at each to admire the finely dressed mannequins, contemplating the attire as if it were in the reach of her empty pocketbook.

"*¡Qué belleza!*" she said, pressing her nose to the glass of a dress shop. A wide-brimmed hat with a purple sash had caught her eye. "That color complements my eyes."

Sonia squinted to read the price tag and gasped.

"We'll have to work until we're old women to buy that," she said. "It's more than a year's worth of wages!"

Eva pouted. "This way, then, spoilsport."

She unbuttoned the top of her uniform to show off her neck and crossed the busy street with confidence. Sonia followed, only narrowly dodging a man maneuvering his heavy vegetable cart over the cobblestones.

"Careful!" he huffed, just as she bumped into the street sweeper, pushing his broom.

"Look where you're walking, *señorita!*" cried the other.

Sonia mumbled her apologies and rushed to catch Eva, who was nearly lost inside the mob of servants dashing about on their early morning errands. All were dressed in the fussy uniforms of the houses they served. Eva knew each house by heart.

"The red shirts belong to the Rodero family, the pale green skirts to Ortiz." She waved at a girl she recognized. "And that bile-yellow sash is an atrocity of the La Calles," she added under her breath. "Even our widow's garb is better than that."

When they finally reached the food market, it was already as crowded as an ant colony. Their strategy was for Sonia to read the items aloud as Eva spied the right vendor and pushed her way to the front of each line. They bought fresh milk and cream, picked tangerines for ambrosia, waited for two loaves of bread to be pulled from the baker's oven, and found cuts of pork that would not become too hard in Dalia's fryer.

By midday their baskets felt heavy, and their backs were soaked with perspiration. The black uniforms seemed to draw in every last ray of sunshine.

"I can't walk another step," Eva groaned, sinking onto a shady bench near a long line of parked cars. She unlaced her heavy shoes and pried them off before rolling down her stockings to cool her legs. "It's no wonder Ramona has such flat feet."

A familiar voice interrupted her. "What's the matter? You girls look like two wilted flowers!"

It was Oscar, the house chauffeur. He looked like a dapper grandfather in his bow tie and cap, leaning against his black car, newspaper under his arm. A round-faced dollop of a man, he often came to the kitchen window in the afternoon to escape the silly conversations of his own young apprentices, who always bragged about girlfriends, fast cars, and horse races.

"Oscar! What a miracle to find you here!" Eva said as he joined them.

"Not really. I've taken *la señora* to her engagement. I won't be needed until the afternoon."

Eva offered a sly smile to Sonia and checked her reflection in the buffed hood. Passersby were admiring the stately automobile, wondering, like Sonia, about the luxuries inside.

"I don't suppose you'd take us home. You can drop us by the back gate so Teresa doesn't see. It's just that the trolley stop is across the plaza. I'll die before I reach it," Eva said.

Sonia held her breath. Tía Neli had told her that something this grand might happen. The only vehicle she'd ever known was Rafael's old truck.

Oscar's laugh was little bursts of steam through his teeth. "Of course, I'll take you. I can't have you perish so stupidly. But if you're not in a hurry, how about a shaved ice first?" He pointed at a bucktoothed young man smiling amiably from his umbrella cart near the fountain. Oscar turned to Sonia and winked as he handed her two coins.

"That's my nephew. He gives pretty girls a good price if they smile."

Sonia stared down at her uniform and then at the healthy flush in Eva's cheeks.

"Maybe you should go, Eva."

But Eva only gave Sonia's hair a little straightening with her fingers. "Give it a try, *amorcito*. Allure is an art; it takes practice."

"*S-s-s-s-s-s!*" Oscar laughed and slapped his knee as Sonia crossed the plaza.

They sat in happy and refreshed silence, enjoying the sights. Workers crisscrossed the busy streets in their smart suits and new shoes. The women left behind a scent of fancy soaps as they whisked by in dresses that only grazed their knees. The men's pastel ties flapped over their shoulders in the breeze.

But it was a group of schoolgirls that caught Sonia's attention in particular. Here in the capital, even people her own age looked special in a way she'd never seen at home. No one wore dusty sandals or walked in bare feet. Their hair was combed and pinned, their skin fresh. They looked regal, Sonia thought admiringly, in their pleated skirts and crisp white shirts, a red kerchief tied at their necks. They held books to their chests, shiny ones filled with new and exciting information, she imagined. How nice to be a girl on the way home for a lunch that was prepared by someone else. How lovely not to be the one toiling over steaks and fried potatoes in a grand kitchen that wasn't her own.

Oscar savored his ice loudly as Sonia watched the group round the corner.

"You know, you remind me of my own granddaughter," he told her finally.

"I thought *I* reminded you of your granddaughter," Eva protested. "You're shameless."

Oscar smiled guiltily and pulled a picture from his wallet.

"This is Lara." He pointed to a girl who looked nothing at all like either one of them. "She dreams of becoming a doctor," he said proudly.

Sonia studied the photograph. Lara looked to be about fifteen, and she had the bright eyes of hope.

"A doctor? That's good, Señor Oscar," Sonia said politely. She did not mention that intelligence meant nothing in Tres Montes, where almost no one finished school, regardless of their talents.

Oscar nodded. "A born intellect. Just like her mother." He looked at Sonia and dabbed the cold syrup from his lips.

"But you have the high forehead of a bright child, too. I see something special behind your eyes."

128

"Not at all, Señor Oscar," she replied quickly. "I'm quite ordinary. I'm happy with dusting and fetching."

"Are you sure?" he asked. "There's not something else you want to be?"

Sonia fell into a thoughtful silence. She only knew what she did *not* want to be. Not magic. Not lonely. Not trapped. Never once had she thought of what she *did* want, never imagined a future the way Lara did.

"Don't strain yourself with all that thinking, *amorcito*," Eva told her. "How many choices do you think there are for girls like us?"

Sonia smiled at Oscar, who was still waiting patiently for her reply.

"I am not sure what I'll be, *señor*. Maybe a teacher." The words sprang to her lips from the blue. She shrugged at Eva, who looked positively shocked. "You have to admit that ours at home is a disaster."

On the ride home, they took turns telling Oscar all about silly Irina Gomez. Sonia marveled at the electric car windows as she listened to Eva's imitations of Irina Gomez.

"It's from the goodness of my heart that I slave with these harlots and dunces," Eva said, throwing back her head. "Not even my doctorate in pedagogy—have I mentioned it?—can break through their thick skulls!"

Oscar's eyes narrowed to watery slits as he laughed at all they said.

What will you be?

Sonia let that question roam through her mind all afternoon after she returned to Casa Masón. In all her life, no one had ever asked her what she hoped to be. They never asked Rafael or Luis or anyone. Irina Gomez certainly hadn't entertained such thoughts. But neither had her parents, though she knew they loved her. Why not?

She was walking back from the laundry, still admiring Lara's audacity, when she saw the rear gates open. This time it was not Oscar's long black car winding through the grounds, but a bright red convertible barreling down the path in her direction. When she looked carefully, she saw that Umberto was behind the wheel.

Sonia stepped on the lawn to let the miniature car pass, but instead it came to a halt right beside her. Umberto looked suntanned, and his hair was tousled. He wore sunglasses and a fine linen shirt that was the same creamy color of the leather seats. From where she was standing, she could even smell his cologne.

"I can never resist stopping for a pretty girl," he said, smiling. "It's my weakness. Hop in. It's Sonia, isn't it? Come on; I'll give you a ride to the main house."

The engine made the ground beneath her feet rumble in a way she did not like. For a moment, she was tongue-tied, thinking of how to escape. The others were back at the kitchen—and she suddenly felt very much alone.

"It's not far, Señor Umberto," she said carefully. "I can walk. But thank you very much for the offer." She started off quickly, but his little car lurched forward.

Umberto took off his glasses and pocketed them before leaning over to open the door. "I insist."

Sonia stared at the door and the two compact seats. How exactly did one refuse a request from her employer's nephew?

"You there!" Teresa was hobbling along the path from the garden, waving her handkerchief like a flag. "Come along!"

Sonia breathed a sigh of relief. For the first time since meeting her, she was thankful to lay eyes on the old woman.

"I'm afraid I have to go," she told Umberto politely.

"Pity," he said, and zoomed off toward the garage.

She ran to where Teresa was waiting up at the path.

"*A la orden*, Señora Teresa," she said, out of breath.

Teresa waited for Umberto's car to disappear before grabbing Sonia roughly by the arm and leading her toward the house.

"What did you think you were doing out there?" she asked through clenched teeth.

"Nothing, Señora Teresa," Sonia said in shock. "I delivered the laundry and was on my way back. Señor Umberto drove up and offered a ride."

Teresa squeezed her arm tighter with surprising strength.

"We don't hire hussies here, you understand? You stay away from that boy."

"Hussy? It's nothing like that! I tried to say no —"

The old woman let out a snort and continued on toward the house. The effort of marching at this pace was making her wheeze.

"I've lived long enough to smell trouble. I know how some of you country girls think! You want to slip inside the eyes of any rich man and snag his imagination, so his money can solve all your problems. You'll throw yourself at anything. *¡Tremenda!*"

Sonia pulled her arm free at last and stopped near the kitchen door. "But that's not true, Señora Teresa. I don't want anything to do with him."

Teresa's eye was twitching.

"You are a domestic," Teresa hissed. "A domestic *apprentice*, in fact, which means you have a place — and that's in the kitchen, understand? You are not paid to fill the eyes of men, least of all Señor Umberto. Stay away from him. If I see you talking again, I'll have you on the next train home. Do you hear me?"

Sonia entered the kitchen without a word.

Ramona looked up from her ledger book and frowned when she saw Sonia's expression. "Is there a problem?"

"Go help the others with the linens," Teresa snapped. "A word with you, Ramona." She motioned to the dining room.

Sonia sat down at the table, where Dalia and Eva were already working. Her lips were trembling, and her eyes were brimming with tears of frustration, already imagining her reputation in shreds.

Eva reached for a napkin and looked over her shoulder. "What's the matter with the old witch now, *amor*?"

Sonia shook her head as her tears spilled. She reached for a napkin to fold.

"Don't worry, *amorcito*," Eva cooed. "One day, when you're a teacher, you won't have to deal with the likes of that old thing—not to mention being spared the trouble making these silly birds." Four cloth swans were already made for the lunch table.

Dalia looked at Eva with disdain. "Why do you do this,

Eva? Let this silly girl feel sorry for herself? Fill her head with pointless dreams? What are you going to tell her next, eh? That one of these birds can take flight?"

Eva kept her eyes down as she worked. "Don't be cruel. Some of us still have feelings, Dalia. We haven't all forgotten how to dream, you know."

Dalia's mouth tightened to a line. "Cruel? How about you? You treat this girl like a pampered hothouse flower. She'll never learn how to survive a single day in the real world. *That's* cruel."

She glanced at Sonia, whose cheeks were now rivers, and shook her head in disgust. "Let me guess: Teresa called you a hussy. She would know—that old cow warmed the bed of Señora Masón's father for years." She twisted the next cloth as if wringing a bird's neck. "In time, you'll be called worse. Now, stop your stupid tears. You've been spoiled long enough, little angel."

CHAPTER 16
La Lavandera

THE CEMENT WASHING tubs stood at the back edge of the property, hidden in the shade of two schefflera trees. Normally, the laundry shed and the outdoor tubs were the realm of two local *lavanderas* who arrived from their homes before sunrise and worked like shadows on the various estates of Punta Gorda, scrubbing shirt collars and underwear until they were fragrant and new.

Sonia stared with gloom at the mountain of dirty dinner linens waiting in the nearby baskets.

"It's only until Umberto is done visiting," Ramona said, trying to cheer her up. "Hand me the hose."

Sonia listened as Ramona explained the steps. To keep her from "tempting Umberto," as Teresa had so plainly put it, Sonia would do the laundry each morning instead.

Only until Umberto is done visiting. And why exactly did she have to pay the price for Umberto's unwanted attentions? Sonia didn't dare ask. All morning she hauled hot water and scrubbed until her nails peeled down like paper.

When she returned to the kitchen for the lunch hour, the front of her uniform was soaked and clinging to her chest.

Eva looked up as Sonia lugged in the basket of pressed linens. She was crushing bulbs of garlic for the *sofrito*.

"Look at it this way, *amorcito*," she whispered when Ramona went to store the laundry in the buffet. "The smell of coconut soap under your nails is better than garlic."

"And why do they have you out here?" Oscar asked as he handed Sonia a clothespin a few days later. He had noticed her in the shadows, where she had been wrestling to pin sheets on the line.

Sonia felt a blush rising. How could she explain those ugly accusations to a grandfather?

"Teresa ordered it," she replied carefully.

"*Ay*, what is that old woman thinking? I'll have a talk with her. A young girl likes to work with her companions— not here with only the lizards for company."

Sonia turned to him, pale. "Please don't." The last thing she needed was to get any more of Teresa's attention. "I don't mind at all. It's . . . nice to be out in the fresh air."

She finished pinning and headed back to the sheets she had left soaking in the basin. Already her shoes were wet and squeaky.

Oscar sat down in the shade and looked out at the rose gardens, thinking. "Well, I suppose it doesn't hurt to learn more than one job. I've done plenty of things here at Casa Masón myself, too — some better than others."

"Oh?"

"You see those rosebushes over there?"

Sonia stopped stirring the clothes with her broom handle and squinted. Roses climbed up a trellis near the gazebo. The heads were large and yellow.

"I planted them myself," Oscar continued proudly. "Grown from seeds, in fact."

"So, you were the gardener?"

He nodded and wiped his forehead with his hand-kerchief.

"Yes, a long time ago, before my back creaked and my knees swelled. That's a job for young men. We old horses get put out to pasture. In my case, I drive and wait, drive and wait." He let out a sigh. "It's a hard thing to grow old and feeble. Much better to be young and full of illusions—and in love." He lowered his voice. "I planted those flowers to impress a young girl, if you want to know the truth. I was always a romantic."

Sonia smiled at him. She was thinking of what Oscar might look like as a young man holding a bouquet. "And *was* she impressed?"

"You could ask her, I suppose."

"Your wife?"

"No, no. Ileana is long dead." He crossed himself. "This was before I knew her. I planted those roses for Teresa." Oscar clapped his hands in delight and threw back his head to laugh at Sonia's surprise. "*S-s-s-s-s-s.* Don't look at me like that; it's true! We weren't always so shriveled and old, you know. She was a beauty once."

Sonia shook her head as she rubbed at a stubborn spot. Oscar had escaped a terrible life with Teresa; that was for sure.

"But what happened? Why didn't she marry you?"

Oscar paused, his smile looking frozen for a moment. Then he waved his hand and shrugged.

"Ah, well, that was long ago," he said vaguely. "There were other . . . circumstances."

Sonia didn't press him further, remembering what Dalia had told her in the kitchen. Teresa had been one of

Señor Masón's mistresses. But now it suddenly occurred to her: Had that been what Teresa wanted? Or had it been what her employer demanded?

"Let's see what's going on in the world today." Oscar sat down nearby and opened the morning paper, squinting over his reading glasses as he surveyed the stories.

After a while he clicked his tongue in disgust. "*Mira para eso.* Such a waste."

Sonia looked up. "What is it?"

He cleared his throat and read aloud what had snagged his attention.

"Since January 1, the medical examiner's office has handled thirty-eight bodies found in different locations in the desert.

" 'We have been picking up between one to four bodies daily since the beginning of the month,' said Doctor Ragoberto Anzuela, chief medical examiner. 'We found one young man just last night. Most of the people we find are recently deceased.' "

Oscar put down the paper and sighed. "So much sadness, just for a chance to work, don't you think, Sonia? And to think it's come to this: all you need is the tiniest bit of money in your pocket and you're a target for any thief!" He looked at her and sprang to his feet. "What's the matter, *niña*? Don't you feel well?"

Sonia had gone pale. Long drips of suds fell from her fingertips to her shoes.

"Does it say who was found?" she asked. A chill spread through her as she thought of Rafael in the desert like Luis. "Is there a name?"

"Just a picture."

She took the paper in her wet hands and studied the image of two masked doctors standing over the latest victim for a long while. The hair was curly. The clothes were not Rafael's. Relieved, she gave the newspaper back to Oscar and turned to the basins without a word.

Oscar watched her carefully. Her hands trembled as she shook out new soap flakes into the water.

"You have a brother, I hear," he said gently. "Eva seems to think he's quite spectacular."

Sonia nodded, her eyes suddenly clouding. "His name is Rafael."

Oscar pursed his lips and stared at his hands.

"In that case, I'm sure he is very smart like you," he told her. "And very good at taking care of himself."

Sonia thrust her arms into the hot water and held her breath against the sting.

"No more dreary stories this morning," Oscar said at

last. "My apologies! I don't know what I was thinking. This is no way to entertain a young lady. I've spent too much time around the mechanics—that's the problem. Those boys live for gore." He checked his watch quickly. "I'll tell you what: I have about thirty minutes before *la señora*'s first appointment. Why don't I run back to the kitchen and get us some cold drinks?"

Without waiting for an answer, he stuffed the newspaper under his arm and started along the path.

CHAPTER 17
Driven to Distraction

"WHAT'S THE MATTER with you, Pancho?" Señor Pasqual demanded. "Stop disgracing me! It's those silly stories of yours, isn't it? You can't dream and drive at the same time!"

Pancho hung his head in shame. He didn't bother to explain the truth behind the accident. Señor Pasqual was a busy man, not a romantic with patience for problems that resulted from the heart. Who could blame him for his bad temper? Pancho had become a distracted and reckless driver, one of the worst in the whole fleet. Only yesterday, he'd forgotten to deliver two packages and later had crushed the toes of an old man resting in the shade. Now this: a turn taken too sharply had pitched his passenger in the road. The victim had been Señor Ruiz—the head of the post-and-telegraph office, no less.

Early that morning Pancho had been driving Señor Ruiz to the plaza for his coffee and newspaper, thinking about Sonia as usual. Moments later Señor Ruiz was bruised and groaning in the road.

Now Pancho looked at his dented handlebars in mortification. It would take a contortionist to steer this bike from now on.

"And don't think for a moment that I'm paying for the repair." Señor Pasqual torqued the handlebars as best he could. "It's coming out of your wages. Now, go! If I hear another complaint, you'll be out."

"It won't happen again, *señor.*"

Pancho pedaled away, but it was no use. Every thought was of Sonia. Once again his distractions got the better of him, and before he knew it, he found himself standing in the shady yard of the Ocampos without a single reason for being there.

Felix and Tía Neli were having a silent breakfast in the yard. Pancho saw at once that the ugly rumors were true. The Ocampo twins had vowed never to speak to each other again. Felix blamed Tía Neli for planting silly ideas in his children's heads; she was angry at his lack of appreciation for her efforts.

"No one called for a taxi," Felix groused when he saw Pancho standing there. "Get on your way."

"Ignore him," Tía Neli said. "Come eat a pastry, Pancho. You look like a starved cat."

Pancho took off his dusty cap and approached with care. The pastry was tempting, but when he reached their table, his eyes fell on something even better. Felix Ocampo was bent over a sheet of paper. From the looks of it, it was a letter to Sonia—or at least a jumble of misspelled words addressed to her.

Felix looked up and glared. "Do you mind? I'm busy."

"Some people are so rude." Tía Neli shook her head and grabbed a pitcher. "Milk?"

"And some people can't butt out of other people's affairs," Felix retorted. "If I want to write to my daughter, I will. Who else can help us?" He scratched out another word until he'd rubbed a hole in the surface. "How do you spell *disappeared*?"

Tía Neli looked at the clouds and did not reply.

"*¿Desaparecido?*" Pancho asked worriedly.

"Yes, *disappeared*. As in 'Your brother has disappeared.'"

Pancho swallowed hard and spelled the word as Felix labored over each letter. Pancho tried not to notice his difficulties. Felix Ocampo was the kind of man who used his word and a handshake to make his deals. He'd probably never set foot in a schoolhouse.

Felix balled up the paper in frustration.

"*¡Vaya. Qué basura!*" he said in disgust.

Pancho thought quickly. "Would you like me to write it down, *señor*? I am a very trusty speller."

Felix looked at him dubiously. "Sit down." He slid a new sheet of paper and the pencil nub across the table. "Take this down exactly."

"Haven't you caused enough trouble for one day?" Señor Ruiz snapped when Pancho appeared at the mail window near midday.

"Señor Ocampo asked me to post this to Casa Masón today." Pancho slid an envelope addressed to Sonia across the counter, wishing he wouldn't have to mail it at all. He could only imagine the sad look on Sonia's face when she received news that Rafael was still missing.

Señor Ruiz took a look at the sad-faced orphan. He smoothed what remained of his hair over the large welt on the side of his head.

"Cheer up, Pancho. I forgive you. I wasn't hurt *that* badly. It's not like you killed me, after all."

"Killed?" Pancho's eyes were wide with alarm. He'd been thinking of Rafael on the whole ride back to town. "Heaven forbid anyone else in Tres Montes should meet such an end, *señor*."

Pancho's stomach growled loudly as he left the post office. *Maybe Mongo would spare a snack,* he thought. He headed to La Jalada and found a shady resting spot at the corner.

He was just parking his taxi when the side door opened unexpectedly. Conchita Fo leaned out, kissing one of her admirers good-bye. Pancho started to turn away—it was none of his business—but then he saw who it was, and he jumped behind a tree to watch. It wasn't just any admirer. It was the police chief—Ernesto Fermín himself—wearing the besotted grin of a schoolboy. Conchita's lips lingered over his doughy earlobes until Pancho grew sick. Ernesto Fermín walked right past him in his happy stupor, never even noticing the boy—or the fact that he'd dropped a lady's handkerchief on the ground. The smell of Conchita Fo's perfume was heavy inside it when Pancho picked it up off the ground.

Who could have guessed? thought Pancho, watching the spring in the chief's step. Ernesto Fermín was married to the mayor's only daughter. He shook his head and checked his watch, realizing how things were. Armando took Señora Fermín to her card game every Tuesday at three. It was precisely 4:35 p.m.

"Are you spying or just skipping out on your taxi job?"

Mongo's voice surprised him. The barkeep was napping

in the shade, a huge machete stuck into the trunk of the tree behind him. He smiled his fearsome grin at Pancho, before reaching for his knife. Then he tossed an orange in the air and sliced it cleanly in two. He offered half to Pancho on the tip of his blade.

"I suppose I don't feel much like working today, Mongo," Pancho said, joining him on the ground.

"And who does?" Mongo replied with a snort. "It would be nice to sit around writing stories all day instead, wouldn't it? Conjuring up whatever world you wanted! Which reminds me: When are you going to finish that pirate story for me? We left off at the plank."

Pancho nibbled on his orange, wishing it were a steak sandwich instead. "Soon. I've been a little preoccupied. I haven't been able to think of the end yet."

"Preoccupied? Oh, I see. Some pretty thing has got your imagination."

Pancho blushed. "Maybe."

Mongo gave him a shove. "Well, do your business and forget her. Women are nothing but a nuisance."

Juice squirted everywhere as Mongo's teeth stabbed through the fruit. He got to his feet and shook his pants clean. "Make sure that ending is bloody and double-crossing," he called as he started to head back inside. "I like excitement."

Pancho licked his sticky fingers, thinking. If only he could make up the world he wanted as Mongo said, he'd have Sonia by his side. Rafael would be safe. People like Conchita Fo and the silly police chief and Señor Arenas would have to answer for their ways.

Too bad real life was much harder than stories. Señor Pasqual would fire him any day now, and Pancho would be forced to sell little verses from a pushcart to keep from starving. Such a waste of a poet's life!

"Get busy, Pancho! There are plenty of fares waiting by the market." It was Armando calling from his own taxi. He was heading the other way with the mayor's daughter. "You don't want Señor Pasqual to hear you've been napping under a tree, do you?"

Pancho waved at his friend, hardly able to look at Señora Fermín, now done with her card game.

"*Buenas tardes, señora,*" he mumbled guiltily as they drove by. It was as if Pancho were cheating on her himself.

CHAPTER 18
A Letter Arrives in the Capital

"IT WAS AN awful scandal," Eva said, savoring the memory like a chocolate morsel. She was quartering onions for the soup, which was to be served with braised beef, white rice, and roasted fowl. Casa Masón had a full calendar of social events and, unfortunately, Umberto—who never liked to miss a day of fun—had decided to stay for a long visit.

Sonia listened intently as she washed rice for the afternoon meal. The kitchen was an oasis from the rest of the house, where she had to work by herself in silence—and now had to be constantly on the lookout for Umberto, who was becoming impossible. Only yesterday he had appeared in the library where she was dusting and encircled her waist, skulking off only when he heard Ramona coming down the hall. She'd made a mental note to check each room carefully before stepping inside.

Eva's eyes had the same dreamy look she wore every evening when she read her torrid love scenes aloud in their bedroom. *No one can make the tantalizing details of someone else's disasters more interesting than Eva*, Sonia thought. It was a true gift. Back home, Eva told stories with such passion that even the victims of her gossip ended up happy with the telling. Today the subject was Teresa, who had once become the unfortunate victim of her employer's attentions. Sonia could hardly believe her ears.

"*Claro*, no one let his wife find out," Eva said. "Or maybe she turned a blind eye. You know how those old-time women were. They expected their men to run loose, so long as they were discreet about it. But everyone knew, just the same."

Sonia bit her lip, listening to the facts: the rumor among the servants of all the estates of Punta Gorda was that Teresa had in fact been young and beautiful once. She had come to replace Katarina Masón's nanny. She'd fallen in love with Oscar, the gardener, but in no time Don Manuel was inviting her into his bed.

Eva sighed and shook her head in dismay. "It must run in their veins," she said. "These pig men want to find pleasure with a country girl and forget her name when things get inconvenient."

"You'd think she'd have some sympathy, then," Sonia

complained. "It's not my fault that Umberto's after me, any more than it was her fault that Señora Masón's father came knocking on her door." She drained the rice through her fingers. "It's not fair."

Eva glanced at Dalia and arched her brow knowingly. Instantly, Sonia felt like a silly child. Dalia slammed her cleaver through a chicken leg, fat splattering from the cutting board. "Not fair? Are there little birds swirling around up there in your head, Sonia? Boys like Umberto aren't punished. You may as well face the ugly facts. If you're stupid enough to think things are fair, then you deserve whatever kind of attention Umberto gives you. Maybe that will teach you to stop being an imbecile."

Sonia stopped what she was doing. "I wouldn't let him touch me that way," she said firmly.

Dalia rolled her eyes. Eva put her hand to her heart. "¡Mi madre! Don't even think of something like that happening to us. What would happen if la señora decides we're too much trouble? They'll call us harlots and send us home. Our families will starve or die of shame — or both! We have to be all eyes around that octopus Umberto!"

Sonia knew they were right. She had a growing stack of money in her drawer that she had promised to wire home for Rafael's truck — and it was very easy to make Teresa cross.

She put the rice on the flame, thinking suddenly of Pancho, whom she'd dreamed of the night before, lying side by side in a field, their arms and legs touching. The memory of it still thrilled her. She liked to imagine his lips pressed warmly against hers and the words he might whisper in her ear as he held her. Pancho was nothing at all like Umberto Masón. She never felt cornered or leered at by him. Still, she wondered how one knew when it was true love and when, as Rafael often said, it was "something else."

"Look what I have here!" The back door opened, and Ramona stepped inside. She was back from market and carried a basket of fresh bread and white cheese. In her hand was a stack of letters.

"The mail!" Eva squealed. "I thought you'd never get back."

She snatched the letters from Ramona and fanned through them. When she handed out the envelopes at last, Sonia felt her heart leap when she saw Pancho's perfect penmanship. What would he say about the note she had left him?

Sonia lifted the seal and started reading. Soon she had to reach for the counter to steady herself.

"*Mi vida*, what is it?" Eva asked, looking up from her mother's letter.

A buzzing noise rose in Sonia's ears as if she were at the ruins once again. She reread the note until the lines grew blurry. Her throat began to close.

"*Niña*, what is it? Is there bad news?" Ramona rushed to take the letter and ease her into a chair.

But Sonia's head was already clouded with a vision.

Rafael's lifeless arms were laid across his chest, mint leaves pressed inside his pallid cheeks. Inside the growing rumble in her ears, Sonia heard neighbors whispering gossip about her parents. "The Ocampos are paying for a sin with their son's flesh."

Eva's voice pierced her stupor as she sat down. "Give me that." She took the letter and read aloud.

"As dictated to Francisco Muñoz by Felix Ocampo.

"Hija,

"Since you left, Rafael has disappeared, and Tía Neli has learned he may have tried to cross to find work. Surely he is in danger, or we would have heard from him by now. Use your prayers to save your brother, Sonia. You are the only hope we have. We depend on you completely."

Ramona sucked in her breath and ran to the pantry. "Dalia, boil water!" She rummaged furiously in a canister for the tea. "A shock like this is serious. My cousin lost six teeth on account of a fright once."

But Dalia did not budge from her spot at the cutting table. Her face was blank; her lips a white line. She pulled another chicken from the pile and took aim.

"Did you hear me?" Ramona said sharply. "Boil the water!"

The cleaver slammed down.

"Damn it!"

Dalia's fingertip was quickly covered in blood. She wrapped it in her apron and cursed, her eyes flashing with angry tears.

"For God's sake, Ramona, how's tea going to help anyone? Least of all Rafael!" she snarled.

With a sharp bang, the door that led to the dining room swung open. Teresa stepped inside. Her opaque eyes were wide and curious. Like a vulture to a carcass, she had followed the scent of discord from the parlor.

"What is this unseemly yelling all about, Ramona?" She looked from one stunned face to the other. "Can't you keep your girls in order?"

Ramona stepped forward. "Forgive us. It's nothing at all, Teresa. Dalia has only nicked herself with the blade. You know young girls. Chatterboxes while they work. All this talk makes them careless." She turned to Dalia. "Go on to the house. Get a bandage. You can see that this accident has made Sonia feel faint."

Teresa clicked her tongue, regarding the vacant expression on Sonia's face, the pale blue of her lips.

"Well, you should all know there's no time for distractions in this house today," Teresa said, sidestepping the spots of Dalia's blood to find the good silver. "There are important things to think about today. *La señora*'s guests arrive in two hours."

Dalia paused near Sonia on her way out. "There was no stopping him; I can promise you that," Dalia whispered in her ear. "Believe me, I tried."

CHAPTER 19

Abuela Comes to Visit

ALL THE REST of the day things were out of sorts. The clocks that Eva had been ordered to wind stopped working without explanation. The gates in the paddock were mysteriously opened, and the frightened horses trampled the vegetable patch.

Even dinner was spoiled. When Ramona brought the cod from the ice chest, she turned away in disgust.

"*¡Ave Maria!* What's this?" she cried. The fish bought fresh that morning was pungent and crawling with maggots.

By night, an awful quiet blanketed La Casita. Dalia stitched the skin on her own finger with a boiled sewing needle and whiskey, seemingly impervious to the pain. Ramona wrote a long letter to her mother and Manuel to remind them of her love. Eva, who could not even calm herself with a book, tossed caution to the wind and lit candles in their room for Rafael. She fastened her hair into pin curls as she watched Sonia for signs of hysterical blindness through the reflection in the mirror.

"You've been counting the spiderwebs for hours, *mi vida*. I can't watch you suffer like this. I think your father is right. Your magic is very strong; everyone knows that. You *can* keep Rafael safe with your prayers. We'll help."

Sonia turned over without a reply.

The night sounds were magnified, and sleep would not come to Sonia's rescue. She listened to the scratching of mice inside the walls, to faint snores, to the moan of the wind, like an old man dying. It rattled the balcony windows, as if a storm were brewing, though all day the sky had been cloudless. Sonia threw her legs over the side of the bed and peered out at the tree branches, silver against the dark purple sky. Then something caught her eye through the glass.

Abuela was standing on the balcony. The old woman's ghost stood with her hands outstretched. Sonia's hair and nightgown whipped behind her as she stepped out on the balcony. The night air felt charged, and it made her shiver, but as she watched Abuela, she caught the comforting scent of Tres Montes after a rain.

"I'm so glad you're here," Sonia told her. "Rafael needs your help."

But her grandmother only shook her head. "You are the only way forward, Sonia," she replied.

Sonia began to cry in shame. "I don't know where my brother is! I can't save him the way people think. You know it's all been a lie."

Abuela took Sonia's hand and pressed something into her palm. It was a small silver key.

"Find the letter," Abuela said. "Then find the Iguana."

"I don't understand. What letter?"

Abuela did not reply. Instead, she began to fade into the darkness.

"Wait!" Sonia cried. "What am I supposed to do?"

But it was no use. Abuela had vanished.

Sonia stepped back inside her room. What could Abuela possibly mean about finding a letter, much less an iguana? She checked quickly. Her father's note was still sitting on her bureau. She sat on the edge of her bed, thinking as she studied the key in the moonlight. It was almost an exact replica of the one she used for her own bedroom door. It had to open something in La Casita, but what door did it fit?

The wind gusted until the curtains billowed like sails. Her bedroom door opened just a crack as if inviting her to the hallway.

Creeping like a cat, she made her way along the dark

hallway to Ramona's door. She slid the key in slowly, but the lock did not budge.

That left only one possibility.

Sonia tiptoed along the creaky floor and put her ear to Dalia's door to listen. Nothing. She put the key in and turned until the bolt made a small *pop!*

"What are you doing?"

Eva was standing behind her, rubbing her eyes.

"Nothing," Sonia whispered.

"It's not *nothing*." Eva stepped closer to get a better look at the key in the lock. "What are you doing with Dalia's key?"

"Looking for something. Go to bed."

"Now I know positively that you're sick with an *espanto*," Eva whispered, trying to pull her back. "If Dalia finds you going through her things like a common thief, she'll kill you."

But Sonia only shot her a warning look and put a finger to her lips as she stepped inside the room. Dalia lay on her stomach, her injured hand hanging over the side of her bed.

"Let's get out of here," Eva urged.

"Shhh!"

The nightstand drawer was empty. Sonia went to the wardrobe. Outside, tree branches clattered against the roof. Sonia could feel Abuela hiding somewhere in the trees, watching.

"Where is it?" Sonia muttered.

"Where is *what*?" Eva whispered. "Who are you talking to?"

Sonia opened the squeaky wardrobe and felt inside the clothes pockets. They were empty.

"Abuela. She came to the balcony. She told me to find a letter, and I know it's in here."

Eva clapped her hands to her mouth. Her frightened eyes scanned the sky outside the window, as if at any moment something might crush her. Sonia knew she hated ghosts almost as much as she loved romance.

Dalia's suitcase was stored on the wardrobe floor. Sonia ran her fingers blindly through the compartments until at last her fingers found something. She held up the envelope triumphantly to the moonlight. Rafael's handwriting was clear.

In a flash, they were across the hall and huddled in Sonia's bed. Eva lit a candle, and Sonia read the letter as quickly as she could in the dim light.

Dalia —

I'll miss your kisses, but when I'm working, I'll come back with plenty of presents for you to make the

wait worth it. Conchita's friend is hiring workers for
his restaurant. It all looks good. Keep an eye on my
baby sister. I trust no one better than you.

Remember me.

Rafael

Sonia's mind raced. So this was the letter. But there was nothing here about a lizard. There was nothing here at all that could help Sonia find Rafael. She could think of only one person who might be able to help her now.

She ran to the window and leaned over the balcony, gauging the drop to the garden below. If she hung from the balustrade by her hands, she could reach the rose trellis. She already had one leg over the railing before Eva lunged after her in a panic.

"Get back here! Where do you think you're going? You can't leave me here with your grandmother's spirit blowing around!"

"I'm going to the main house to make a phone call. I have to find out who Conchita Fo sent Rafael with."

But Eva only pulled back harder.

"Using *la señora*'s phone without permission? No! It will be trouble for all of us if you're caught, and I can't risk my hide for you, Sonia. You're staying right here, *mi amor*," Eva said. "Don't make me wake Ramona."

Sonia thought quickly and rushed back inside. She dug through her closet until she found the fancy shoes Tía Neli had given her as a traveling gift.

"Take these," Sonia said, holding up the high-heeled shoes. "My aunt says they're wonderful for dancing."

The heels were stacked, the toes pointed and shiny. Eva hesitated.

"Take them," Sonia urged. "Take them and say nothing. I'll be back in a little while — I swear it on Luis's grave."

Moments later Sonia stole across the damp grass in her white nightdress. From the balcony it seemed to Eva that her friend's feet were barely touching the ground. She shuddered to see that the girl moved like a ghost herself.

CHAPTER 20

A Call for Help

THE PARLOR DOORS were already open when Sonia arrived,
as though she'd been expected in the eerie purple room.
Her bare feet felt cold against the tile as she crept toward
the phone on the desk. At this hour, the chairs looked
like hunchbacks, the clock on the mantle like the face of a
demon.

Sonia stared at the phone, trying to decide how best to
reach Pancho—not that there were many options. There
were only three telephones in all of Tres Montes to choose
from: one at the telegraph office, another with Señor
Arenas, and the third at the police station. At this hour of
the night, only the police station would have anyone there
who could fetch Pancho from his bed.

It took six rings before a young man's sleepy voice came
on the line.

"Police." Static crackled through the line. "Hello?"

"Yes, yes, I'm here," Sonia stammered.

"Who is calling?"

"This is Sonia Ocampo. Is that you, Tomás?"

Tomás Melendez was the police chief's apprentice, a boy not much older than Sonia.

"Sonia Ocampo?" Another series of crackles sounded. "Speak up," he said. "You sound a million miles away."

"I *am* a million miles away—or very nearly. I'm working in the capital."

"What's the matter, then, for you to be calling in the middle of the night?"

A sound behind her made Sonia turn to listen. Nails against tile floor and a faint whine: the greyhounds were wandering nearby. She cupped her hand over the receiver and lowered her voice further.

"Listen carefully, Tomás. I need to speak to a friend of mine. It's very urgent. Can you find him for me at this hour? I'd be grateful forever."

"Who is it?"

"Pancho Muñoz . . . from school. He lives with Señor Pasqual now. He's—"

"Pancho Muñoz? The orphan?"

"The *taxi boy*." There was no time to argue. "Can you find him quickly? I can call back in exactly ten minutes."

Tomás hesitated. "I don't know, Sonia. Is this urgent business? This is a police station, after all. Capitán Fermín wouldn't like me lending his phone for social calls."

"For God's sake, Tomás. Do you think I'd call to chat at this hour? Now, stop dallying, please. I'll call back in ten minutes."

She hung up the phone and crawled under the desk to wait.

Ten minutes later, Pancho picked up the phone on the first ring.

"Sonia! Is that you? What's wrong?"

Static crackled loudly, but Sonia could make out his voice. For the first time since reading her father's letter, she felt a ray of hope.

"Pancho! Forgive me for waking you in the middle of the night. I hate to ask this, but you said I could call you if I ever needed anything. I need your help now."

"I'll do anything. What do you need?"

"I need to know about my brother's disappearance." There was a long pause on the other end of the line as Sonia listened to the pops and fizzles. "Hello? Are you still there?"

"Yes," Pancho whispered. "I'm sorry."

"Listen carefully," she continued. "I have a question."

"Sonia, I—"

"What do you know about iguanas?"

"What?" he blurted out.

"Iguanas! Like the lizard."

"Nothing; everything." Pancho stammered. "Is *that* the question?"

"Yes."

"Ah." He sounded strangely relieved. "But what does *that* have to do with helping you? I don't understand."

"I wish I knew! It's that Rafael is missing, and Abuela has just come to see me about it. She told me to find an iguana. Oh, I don't know. It's all a mess. All I know for certain is that Conchita Fo made his arrangements. Please, Pancho, see what you can find out."

"But—"

Sonia sat up and listened. There was whimpering next door and the sound of shuffling.

"Sonia?" Pancho's voice was still coming through the receiver. She hung up just as the door swung open.

CHAPTER 21
Men of Loose Morals

THE GREYHOUNDS BOUNDED in, jumping up at her. Sonia let out a tiny yelp.

Smiling in the doorway—and admiring the silhouette of her figure through her thin nightdress—was Umberto Masón.

"Imagine finding a pretty prowler in the middle of the night. Were you sleepwalking, or am I the one dreaming?" he asked a little too pleasantly. He was still in a dress shirt and black pants, recently returned, she assumed, from one of his parties.

Sonia felt his eyes on her breasts. She crossed her arms and kept her eyes trained on him as he walked slowly in her direction.

Umberto gave her a knowing look as he spotted the phone nearby.

"What are you doing here barely dressed? Not that I'm complaining."

Sonia's tongue felt too thick to move.

"No, you don't have to answer," he said, shrugging. "I think I can already guess. It's terrible to find yourself alone in bed. You were in my aunt's parlor making calls to your boyfriend to help you feel better. *Without* permission. Yes?"

Sonia could smell the cigars and scotch on his clothes.

"Don't worry," Umberto continued, smiling. "My aunt has many silly rules. Your secret is safe with me. In fact, all of you is safe with me."

Sonia forced herself to speak.

"It's not what you believe, Señor Umberto," she whispered. "I'm sorry to have taken such liberties. I needed to call home right away; there's been an emergency."

"Oh?" He was staring again at her necklace, at the buttons on her nightdress, at the points of her breasts through the fabric. "What's the emergency?"

Here Sonia fell silent. How could she explain about Rafael, about Abuela?

"It was silly," she said finally. "A misunderstanding that's all resolved now. I'll go. Thank you again."

She started toward the open patio doors when his hand

grazed her waist and pulled her back. She could feel the heat of his palm through her nightdress, but it was not at all a comfort. Nothing like the way she imagined Pancho's hand would feel on her waist.

"I have to go," she said.

"What's the rush? It's a lovely night, isn't it?"

Sonia's heart quickened as his long fingers drew upward along her arms. Outside the wind gusted fiercely, snapping branches in the yard. Flash lightning lit the sky. The dogs, meanwhile, had dropped down and were growling at something outside.

"Please stop, Señor Umberto," she said, stepping back. His sour breath repelled her. "I don't want this. I should get back home. Eva is a light sleeper. If she wakes, she'll be worried."

But Umberto only moved closer. He pressed her close to the wall, and all at once his hands were around her waist and his tongue slid along her neck. Sonia pushed with all her might, but she was useless against the weight of his body as he tried to lift her nightdress over her thighs.

Suddenly, a gust of wind shot through the yard and caught the patio doors, banging them open hard enough so that glass shattered in an explosion. The shards pierced

Sonia's bare feet and arms. Umberto released her instantly, yelping and trying to pull the glass pieces from his cheeks. Almost immediately there were footsteps and shouts from all directions.

Oscar and the gardeners appeared in the yard, holding sticks.

"Sonia?" Oscar asked, his eyes darting warily from Umberto to Sonia. "What's wrong? Are you all right?" He stepped forward and took her arm. "Tell me the truth, *niña*. What's happened?"

The light snapped on inside the parlor, and the room went bright. Sonia felt as though she were caught in a spotlight on a stage. She squinted to see who had arrived in the doorway.

"Go back to bed, Oscar," Teresa hissed. "I'll handle this."

She was holding an antique pistol in a shaking hand.

CHAPTER 22
A Night for Answers

PANCHO LOOKED THROUGH the open window and saw Conchita laughing at the bar. Glassy-eyed admirers surrounded her and toasted her beauty.

"Are you sure you want to go in there, Pancho?" Armando, who had followed Pancho all the way to La Jalada, pointed at the bar and squinted to get a better look. "It's the middle of the night, and even Mongo looks like he's waiting for someone to kill. *¡Jesucristo!* Look at that cannibal!"

A cleaver went hurtling toward the wall.

"Don't be silly," Pancho said. "He's just playing darts."

Armando's eyes grew wide as he ducked back down.

"Have you finally gone crazy, Pancho Muñoz? It's bad enough you've been driving like a lunatic for days. Then you run off to the police station in your underwear to take a phone call in the middle of the night. Now this! What's between your ears?"

"The only thing that's ever been there: imagination," Pancho said honestly. "Hopefully, that will do."

Armando thumped his friend on the side of the head. "Imagine this, then, you fool: Señor Pasqual's face when he finds out you're hanging around with these drunks instead of picking up fares to pay him back for your bike repairs."

Pancho gave Armando an impatient look. "Then, don't tell him."

"Won't you at least tell me what we're doing here if it's not to pick up a fare?" Armando pleaded. "None of this makes sense! If nothing else, I want to be able to tell Señor Pasqual *why* you were killed when we find your body."

Pancho reached for the door and took a deep breath.

"Of course I won't tell you. Some things are private. Now, go home, Armando, and get some sleep. I'll be fine."

Then he stepped into the bar.

Look calm, Pancho told himself as he crossed the smoky room, but fear was already crawling up his back. It was one thing to venture here in daylight to trade a snack for a story with Mongo, but at night La Jalada drew fearsome men who'd long ago forgotten how to be good. He took note of the arsenal of pistols and knives in plain sight and headed toward the bar without anyone stopping him. For once in his life, Pancho was glad to be the kind of boy no one ever noticed.

Just as he reached his stool, a blade went buzzing past his head and sank into the bull's-eye across the room.

"Good throw, Mongo," Pancho said, sliding onto a bar stool. He checked to make sure his ear was still attached. A shiny collection of cutlery sat on the bar.

The barkeep put down the knife he was aiming and turned with a look of surprise.

"What are you doing here at this time of night? This is no place for you. Be smart and get out," he said.

"But I brought you the end to the pirate tale." Pancho pulled a folded sheet of paper from his shirt pocket and held it in the air.

"Are you playing or not?" someone called.

Mongo hurled a dagger at the man's feet in reply.

"Back here, my friend," he told Pancho.

When Pancho's snack and tale were finished—and the sea captain was beheaded and fed to the sharks as the outlaws cheered—Mongo looked as satisfied as if he'd eaten a heavy meal.

"Excellent," he said, picking his teeth. "Your best one yet. Maybe drag out the sword fight just a tad."

"Good point." Pancho glanced over his shoulder nervously. "I have another reason I wanted to talk to you alone, Mongo."

"Well, then. Out with it." Mongo leaned forward to listen.

Pancho knew he couldn't ask about Rafael directly. It would violate his taxi boy oath completely. He hated to lie to Mongo, but what choice did he have?

"I want to arrange a trip north," he whispered. "I'm tired of being a taxi boy. Señor Pasqual works us like oxen, and there's no future in it. I'd rather take my chances someplace else."

Mongo sat back and shook his head.

"Be smart and go to Arenas, then," he said. "It won't be quick, but it will be better. Trust me." He stood to go.

"Better than what?" Pancho asked, grabbing him by the arm. It felt like stone beneath his fingers. "Why can't Conchita Fo help me? I hear she has contacts."

"Don't be nosy, and go see Arenas." Mongo pulled away and looked over his shoulder cautiously. "It's getting late. You should get out of here."

"No," Pancho said firmly. "I'm going north, Mongo. If you won't help me, I'll speak to Conchita Fo myself. She'll know someone who can take me over quickly." Here he paused. "Perhaps someone who is not too expensive."

Mongo's fierce look made Pancho's knees quiver. The barkeep's voice was a deep growl.

"I don't like to repeat myself to brats who think they know everything. Get that idea out of your head before you're sorry. You'll never see the north if you arrange with her."

"Why not?" Pancho asked. "Tell me what happens to the boys she sends."

"For God's sake, Mongo, there are thirsty men out there and no one to serve them!" Conchita Fo was standing at the beaded curtain. She took one look at Pancho and frowned. "Get your food someplace else! Out!"

Mongo closed his fist around Pancho's collar.

"He was just leaving." He dragged Pancho out the back door like a sack of trash.

"Please listen, Mongo. I *have* to know."

For a moment, he was sure he had failed. Mongo pressed him roughly against the wall.

"You have to know? Then listen. They end up crying for their mothers like rats eating onions—if they make it out at all. They think they're going to her friend's restaurant in the north. But there's no friend, you understand? There's only her man, the one they call Iguana. She collects the fare—and he waits in the valley to rob them of the rest of what they've got. Lambs to the slaughter, Pancho. No one should be so cursed. Now, get out, and never let me see you here again at night, or I'll kill you myself."

The door slammed, and Pancho was all alone in the dark alley.

CHAPTER 23
Pancho's Escape

"HOW DARE YOU break into my place of business! Get up and find someplace else to sleep," Carmen scolded as she shook Pancho awake with her foot.

He bolted up from his sleep and banged his head on the desk drawer. Pancho had picked the lock on Señor Arenas's office and fallen asleep beneath Carmen's desk as he waited for morning.

"We're not running a shelter for vagrants!" Carmen continued. "Out!"

"Thank goodness it's you, Señorita Carmen!" He stood up and peered out the window. His bike taxi was still hidden under branches, where he'd pushed it out of view the night before.

"Stop trying to flatter me. Of course it's me. I'm here every day, unfortunately." Carmen threw open the shutters and frightened off the roosting doves. "You orphans—you can't help but behave like criminals, I guess! I have a mind to call the police chief though."

"No! Don't do that, *por favor*," Pancho said quickly. Conchita Fo's *amor*? It would be a disaster. He followed on Carmen's heels.

"A million pardons, but I've come to beg a favor."

Carmen turned and put her hands on her hips.

"The nerve."

"I need to reach Sonia Ocampo in the capital," Pancho continued quickly. "It's an emergency. I was hoping you'd give me the number and allow me to use the telephone."

Carmen's mouth dropped open, and she rolled her eyes to the heavens.

"Emergency, eh? What is it? Are you dying of yearning? Unfortunately for you, young man, a broken heart does not qualify as an emergency around here. You think Sonia Ocampo is on vacation in the capital? She's *working* as a representative of Señor Arenas. She is not to be distracted by her lovesick boyfriend."

He tried not to blush at the word *lovesick*, though he might as well admit it. *Love* was the only thing that could name the odd feeling pressing on his chest at night, the way he hugged his pillow, the urge that made him whisper Sonia's name just to hear it spoken.

"I beg you, Señorita Carmen—"

She held up her hand in warning.

"But it's a life-or-death matter!" Pancho persisted. He looked over his shoulder and lowered his voice. "It involves Rafael Ocampo."

Carmen paused. "The miner?" she asked, her cheeks flushing. "Why should I care about him?"

Pancho could see that he wasn't the only lovesick soul in these mountains.

"You should care because you are a good and kind person, Señorita Carmen, and you would not let anything happen to Rafael just because he did something foolish. Rafael may be in danger."

"Danger?" She narrowed her eyes. "What do you mean?"

"Please, *señorita*. You know I'm a taxi boy. We have certain oaths; I would have to break them to tell you. You'll have to trust me when I say that I must speak to his sister at once. You are smart enough to know that a letter will be too slow to reach Sonia in the capital. I *must* use the telephone." He got down on his knees and reached for her hand. "Won't you help me? It will be our own secret. We will be finished before Señor Arenas even arrives."

"You think so?" a deep voice said.

Pancho's stomach lurched as he turned to find Señor

179

Arenas breathing down his neck. The man's mouth smelled strongly of old whiskey and eggs. Carmen stared at her hands as he fumed.

"Didn't I tell you not to lurk around here?"

This was no time for fear. Pancho swallowed hard and stood his ground.

"I'm not lurking, *señor*. I came to have a word with Señorita Carmen."

Señor Arenas sized him up—but kept his hands to himself.

"Don't come back again, or I'll have Ernesto Fermín lock you up with the rats! Be gone in two minutes, or I'll send for him."

He stormed past Carmen and disappeared inside his office.

"Look what you've done!" she cried to Pancho as she shooed him out the door. "He'll be in an ill humor all day, thanks to you!"

The door slam echoed down the street.

With a heavy heart, Pancho dug out his taxi and rode off. There had to be a way to reach Sonia and tell her what he had learned about the Iguana and Rafael's doomed journey through the valley. It was their only hope to save him. For a moment, he thought he might try Señor Ruiz at the telegraph office, but he'd have to pay for the service — completely out of the question with his empty pockets.

The whistle of the morning train broke his thoughts. Pancho checked his watch and pointed his taxi by habit toward the railway stop. The train would be crossing the last bridge and would pull into the station in a few minutes. Already the ground was rumbling with its approach in the distance.

Suddenly, Pancho saw a pinhole of light in his problem. As the train's headlights drew closer, a bright new idea lit his mind. He pumped his legs madly until his taxi's wheels squeaked loudly in protest. He raced with all his might toward the stop.

Did he dare?

To the capital?

Without Señor Pasqual's permission?

All these doubts and more plagued him, but he rushed to the rail stop anyway and moved his taxi carefully into the shade at the far end of the station, where he hoped Señor Pasqual might find it later. He took Sonia's letter from its hiding spot beneath the worn springs and frowned at his empty pockets. Then, like a monkey, he scampered high inside a tree to wait.

✣ ✣ ✣

Hours later Marco stood at the top of the aisle.

"*!Atención, señores!* Have you tickets in your lap . . ." he began.

Pancho didn't move a single muscle as he huddled in the bathroom. Through the crack of the door, he could see the conductor moving down the aisle, punching holes in passengers' tickets.

I'm coming, Sonia, he thought, pressing his hand against her letter, safe in his breast pocket.

The whistle screeched as they slowly pulled out of the station.

CHAPTER 24
An Old Lovers' Quarrel

"LISTEN TO REASON, woman," Oscar whispered to Teresa. "You know as well as I do that the boy is a lecher."

It was early morning. Oscar had taken the liberty of scooping up the freshly delivered newspaper from the gate and knocking on Teresa's door to hand it to her. Of all the servants, she was the only one with quarters in the main house. Her small bedroom was at the back of the first floor beyond what had once been the nursery. She had lived in the old nanny's room since her youth.

"Don't you presume to tell me what I can do, Oscar. I won't have it." Teresa sat on the edge of her chair, her knotty hands folded on the paper as she regarded the chauffeur stiffly. "The girls in this house are my affair, not yours."

Oscar sighed. Sonia had refused to utter a word about why she'd come to the library in the first place, but whatever the reason, he was sure Umberto Masón had not been part of the girl's plan.

"Yes, that's true, the girls are your business," he said. "But I know Masón men. You were a girl once, Teresita," he told her. "Or don't you remember?"

Teresa gave him an iron look. "I remember quite exactly."

He stepped away from the door, where he had been standing, cap in hand, and pulled a wooden chair next to hers. Slowly, he covered her bony hands in his.

"All I'm saying is that a Masón ruined a chance for happiness of two people once. Why should another life be ruined?"

Teresa closed her eyes, but her voice was strong.

"I'm not a miracle worker, Oscar. I can fire her or let her get bedded by that louse — one of the two. Which would you rather have?"

Oscar stared at the delicate fingers of her hands, remembering how lovely they had been long ago.

"Neither one, Teresa. But I have an idea."

CHAPTER 25
The Stowaway

"WAIT! PLEASE! I have to get to the capital! It's urgent!" Pancho shouted.

The baggage clerks holding his arms were unsympathetic. They held him, struggling, as Marco, the brass pins of his uniform gleaming, kicked open the side door.

"Toss the little stowaway," he ordered.

Pancho pressed his legs as hard as he could against the door frame. Tall pine trees whizzed by in a black blur as the train climbed the mountain.

"Marco, *por Dios!* What are you saying? It's me: Pancho, from home! Please permit me to explain!"

Until a few moments earlier, if anyone had asked him about the ride to the capital, Pancho might have said it was most pleasant. But now, discovered asleep in his hiding spot and about to be pushed from a moving train, he was terrified.

Struggle as he might, he was no match for the brutes who dislodged his feet. They swung him to and fro like a sack. Marco, impervious to Pancho's pleas, gave a nod.

"Explain that to the hungry panthers," he called as Pancho went sailing high in the air.

Pancho was soon rolling uncontrollably down the rocky pitch. A boulder near the river stopped him with a thud.

He lay winded for some moments, counting his teeth with his tongue and wondering about his new life as a cripple. But then, because he remembered the large cats that roamed the countryside, he sat up, wincing, and took inventory of his pathetic state. He was alone in the middle of the Haunted Valley, miles away from his destination. He had no money. And, from the strange angle of his sore shoulder, he was sure his arm had been pulled loose from its socket.

A long whistle sounded. He turned just in time to see the train disappear around a bend in the hillside.

Now what? he asked himself fiercely.

How foolish to have fallen asleep during the very last leg of the trip! He had managed to stay hidden for the first part, excusing himself and pretending to be a traveler each time a surprised passenger opened the door to find him. Despite all this, sleep had claimed him, and in the end a large woman suffering from stomach cramps had been his undoing. She had found him curled near the toilet and screamed for help. He could still feel the sting of her shouts in his ears.

Pancho would have to walk the remaining thirty kilometers to the capital. He squeezed his eyes shut and did the calculations, never his best skill. It would take a laborious ten hours if he hurried, and he would probably have to walk the last three of those after nightfall. He tried not to think about panthers or the howler monkeys watching from the vines above. The monkeys were an unfriendly lot that threw their excrement at intruders, but the black cats were much worse. Their fearsome growls reverberated through the night air like thunder.

When he was done feeling sorry for himself, Pancho dusted off and started up the hill. At least he still had the gift of strong legs.

The sun grew hot as Pancho trudged along, following the train tracks for guidance as best he could. He ate the meat pie he had filched from a passenger's bag some time back, and when that was finished, he took to eating the berries that he saw birds pecking at, which he assumed meant they weren't poisonous. Each time he grew parched, he listened for water and found creeks to drink from. He cooled his throbbing feet and stuffed leaves in his shoes as the soles began to give way like wet paper.

He walked along for hours, singing and telling himself stories, thinking of Sonia, but his spirits were dying as quickly as the daylight. He hurried his steps and kept his eyes on the winding tracks to keep from imagining the long distance that remained.

He had finished going around a series of sharp bends when he was stopped abruptly by the disheartening sound of rushing water. When he lifted his gaze, he confirmed the worst. Pancho was looking across an enormous canyon. All that spanned the impasse was a precarious train bridge.

To cross it would be madness, he reasoned, looking down at the foaming river below. There would be nowhere to keep safe from an approaching train, especially not with an injured arm. He looked with defeat at the long terrain he would have to navigate without anything to guide him. The detour would add several more hours to his journey, and nightfall was near. It would be morning before he ever reached the city—*if* he reached it at all.

188

Entrusting his soul to guardian angels, he walked toward the trees. Already the howler monkeys were shrieking their complaints. A lump of feces hit his back.

It was as the moon rose that Pancho became aware of two things. First, he was terrible at navigating by stars. Second, he was not alone.

At first he worried it might be ghosts trying to unsettle him, but the smell of burning wood seemed too real to be imagined, and he was starting to feel chilly. Nearly sprinting, he followed his nose until he found a glowing campfire. He hid himself in the trees to see who had built it.

He saw several pelts, a tin cup and plate, and a worn leather pouch filled with an impressive collection of hunting knives that had apparently been put to use; two skinned rabbits were skewered on the fire. A horse was snorting softly nearby.

All at once, a ferocious growl sounded behind him, and Pancho was thrown to the ground. He prepared for a panther's fangs to pierce his neck, but instead he was pinned by someone who held a sharp blade to his back.

"¡Ay! Have mercy!" Pancho screamed. The pressure against his arm was demonic. His ears buzzed and his scalp grew cold. Silver dots floated before his eyes. "My arm is broken!"

At the sound of his cries, the attacker stopped and dragged him, grunting, toward the flames. Pancho was sure he'd be seared alive like another rabbit on the pit, but the brute only heaved him into the light to have a good look.

Pancho stared in disbelief at the face gaping before him. His head went icy and his mouth limp. Several faces swirled before his eyes.

"It's you!" he said weakly.

Then the world went black.

CHAPTER 26

A Friend on the Road

PANCHO AWOKE INSIDE a dry tent. He sat up and found that his arm, though still throbbing, was now set properly in a sling.

He stuck his head out of the flap and saw someone leaning over the fire. It had not been a dream after all.

Mongo was sharpening his knives. He caught Pancho's reflection in the curved blade.

"Imagine running into you here, kid." He made another long swipe and chuckled.

Pancho stepped out of the tent, relieved though his knees were still a bit unsteady.

"Thank God it was you, Mongo. I was sure it was the end." He looked around at the horse and the tidy campfire. "But what are you doing here in the middle of La Fuente?"

"I could ask you the same," Mongo replied. "I can see you didn't like my advice about seeing Arenas."

"No," Pancho admitted. "But really, what are you doing here?"

"Trying to keep you alive and out of trouble, of course."

"Oh." Pancho felt his cheeks get warm in a pleasant sort of way. "How did you know where to look?"

"I'm only ugly, Pancho, not dumb. They found your bike at the station, and I added things up." He examined his blade in the sunlight. "I thought you might need some company out here. This is no place to be alone." He glanced at Pancho's torn shirt and pants. "From the looks of it, someone has been trying to kill you already."

"Kill me? Not exactly. I . . . fell off the train."

Mongo crossed his arms and grunted. He looked feral in the woods, even more ferocious than he had throwing knives inside La Jalada.

"Did I ever mention that men have died for lying to me?" he asked evenly.

"In that case, I was pushed off the train."

"That's better." He took a long swig of water from a jug. "So, what? Were you trying to rob it? It takes special skill, you know. It's not for amateurs."

Pancho's mouth fell open. "Rob the train? Certainly not!"

192

Mongo pulled another knife across his stone and smiled. "Well, if you weren't robbing the train, why did they toss you?"

Pancho hesitated.

"Speak!"

"I have an urgent errand in the capital but no money to get there. I had no choice but to stow away."

"No choice?" Mongo stabbed his knife into the ground. "Don't bother with lamentations about choice. There's not a man in the whole world who has all the choices he wants. A man can steal because he's starving, but they'll jail him just the same. The sooner you learn that, the better."

Pancho gave this some thought.

"I was on the way to the capital to see Sonia Ocampo."

"Ah," Mongo said, flashing his pointy-tooth smile. "You're after a woman. How original. Didn't we talk about this?"

Pancho's cheeks burned even hotter than before. "It's not like that . . . well, not exactly. I'm . . . I'm trying to save her brother, as a matter of fact."

Mongo stared in shock at Pancho's thin limbs and worn shoes; then he burst into a guffaw. His laughter shook the branches as he doubled over to catch his breath.

"You?" he snorted. "Your face is still smooth! You've

barely grown out of your pigeon chest!" He made rude cooing noises and burst into another long wave of laughter.

Pancho pulled back his sore shoulders.

"I'm not completely powerless, either," he said over Mongo's racket. "As you may remember, I'm a poet. We're a clever lot, if a poor one. I've gotten this far, haven't I?"

Mongo held his sides and wheezed even harder. Finally, he wiped his eyes and looked with wonder at Pancho's resolute expression.

"Is this one of your stories? Because if so, it is a wonderful comedy."

"I'm serious, Mongo. I must get to the capital to see Sonia Ocampo. Her brother is Rafael Ocampo. You know him. You told me yourself that he's probably left with one of Conchita Fo's drivers to meet Iguana."

Mongo sobered at once at the name. He picked at his nails with the tip of his knife. "He sold himself to the devil, then." He motioned his friend to come closer. "There's very little time. So tell me, how much do you know about kidnapping?"

CHAPTER 27

A Surprise in the Garden

"*¡Necia!* You're so clumsy. Pick that up!"

Sonia startled as Teresa snapped her fingers in front of her face. She'd been lost in another daze.

There were many severe punishments possible, Teresa had explained in her fury that afternoon.

"But I know what will fix you," she'd hissed. "It's time I took you in hand. For the rest of your time here, you are to be by my side as if you're tied there, do you hear me?"

Sonia stared now at the mess on Señora Masón's bedroom floor. In her distraction, she had forgotten to balance the velvet jewelry tray. Señora Masón was dressing for a formal dinner at the social club. Her collection of emeralds and pearls was now scattered at Sonia's feet, which were still bandaged from the encounter with Umberto two nights ago.

"A million pardons, *señora.*" She stooped to collect the mess.

Teresa snatched a choker and matching earrings from her hands.

"How did we ever end up with such a disaster of a girl?" she said, slipping the gold posts through Señora Masón's lobes. "Arenas has clearly forgotten our standards."

But Sonia was barely listening. She was already lost in thought again, remembering Rafael's teary face the first day he'd followed their father into the mines. Teresa gave her a pinch that made her jump.

"Do you hear what's been said? You ought to be ashamed!"

"A million pardons," Sonia mumbled. "I was—"

Teresa waved off further explanation.

"You were thinking of things that do not concern anybody," she snapped. "You've had the look of a dead fish all night!"

Sonia closed her mouth and pretended not to hear the rest of the complaints that Teresa hissed in her ears. It was true enough about her appearance. She had had no appetite all day, and so she felt faint and her eyes were dull. But how could it be otherwise? Rafael was crowding every thought, and when he wasn't, it was Umberto who worried her to distraction. She hadn't seen him since their encounter in the library. At any moment he could return and tell his aunt a terrible lie. As far as Sonia knew, Señora Masón had no idea of what had happened.

Teresa pulled out the drawer of the vanity and held out a small brass key.

"Put this box in the top drawer," she ordered, handing Sonia the jewelry case. "You can manage that without dropping things, can't you?"

Katarina Masón chuckled. "I think the sight of all this jewelry is making her nervous," she said. "Calm yourself, girl." She held up her hair to let Teresa fasten her choker. "Did Umberto say when he was coming back?"

Teresa fumbled with the clasp.

"No, *señora*, he didn't."

"I'd hoped he could join me tonight. I have a girl in mind for him — have I mentioned it? The colonel's daughter. A little homely, but she'll run a good house, and her people are well connected. My brother's son needs someone steady, not this string of harlots who are always throwing themselves at him in bars."

Teresa's face was red with frustration as she worked the delicate clasp.

"Caldera is half a day's drive from here, *señora*. Remember? I don't expect he'll be back soon. You know how young men are about their cars."

Katarina Masón shook her head. "I don't know what we're coming to. Vandals are going to ruin this city! Imagine having the nerve to break in to someone's home to destroy things! First my library and then the garage! Oscar said they made a mess of Umberto's car. I'm going to have to hire private guards for the grounds before long."

She looked impatiently at Teresa in the reflection. The old woman's hands were shaking too badly.

"Niña," she called. "Come and do this for Teresa."

Sonia set the box down slowly and went to her employer. Teresa gave her a warning look as she handed over the emeralds.

"Oscar's mechanics tried their best to fix Señor Umberto's car, *señora,*" Teresa said. "But these European models are so complicated—especially for those simple-tons. Don't worry, though. Oscar has assured me his man in Caldera will have the auto like new in a week or two. He is the very best mechanic in the country, I'm told, though he does require that Umberto be on hand to approve the repairs. Naturally, he wants to be sure his most important customer is happy with the work."

Sonia hooked the gold latch, her own hands fighting to keep steady. So this was how the broken window had been explained. It had never occurred to her that the old crone might actually be saving her from doom. But here it was, plain as day. Teresa was lying about everything, and Oscar was helping.

"Finish up already, *niña*, and put the jewelry box away," Teresa ordered. "How many times do I have to say it? We're pressed for time." She stepped behind the lacquered screen with Señora Masón.

Sonia opened the lilac-scented drawers to place the jewelry box among the French intimates folded there. The box was almost too pretty to touch with hands that peeled garlic and swept dirt, Sonia thought. Its ebony cover was inlaid with dragons of ivory and jade from the Forbidden City.

She couldn't resist lifting the lid. Inside was a mesmerizing collection: ruby chokers, rings of amethyst, emerald pendants, and gold bangles. The sight made her jealous, though not for the jewels themselves. A person who owned gems like this would never have to work as a servant or say, *"Sí, señora; no, señora,"* or put up with a toad like Umberto. She wouldn't have to worry a single night about making her family hungry or losing a brother to the lure of a better life.

She replaced the lid carefully, slid the drawer shut, and locked it.

"Is there anything else?" she asked, peering out the

window. The moon was already rising—bloodred. It was the kind of sight that made mothers in Tres Montes close their shutters.

"Put the key in the vanity," Teresa said from behind the screen. "Lock the balcony before you go, too. It's been a busy season for crooks in the capital," she added hastily. "They'll slit a decent woman's throat in her bed without a care."

Sonia paused at the back door and clapped her hands for the dogs. Though Teresa had been with her all day since her encounter with Umberto, she was reluctant to cross the grounds alone at all, especially now when the light made the garden statues glow so garishly. The dogs, however, were nowhere to be found. They'd grown skittish themselves since the night in the parlor and wandered with their tails like scythes between their legs.

She hurried along in the brisk night air, but when she rounded the pond, she found she couldn't take another step. La Casita had come into view. The bedroom windows of the house were already glowing with candles, in Rafael's honor. It was Eva's act of friendship, but Sonia could not bear to look at the flames.

"Don't light them." She tried to take the matches from Eva. The night before, she'd seen sinister shadows on the walls in the candlelight. She was sure she'd seen Luis reaching his arms to her. "We could be forgetful. We could burn alive."

But Eva had persisted just the same, and the smell of melting beeswax had reminded Sonia of all the unanswered prayers—of just how little she could do to help Rafael. She had nightmares until dawn.

Sonia climbed across the footbridge and sat down, legs dangling near the surface of the pond. From her pocket she drew out her pouch of *milagros* and poured the silver pieces into her lap. Mouths, eyes, fists, girls, boys, houses. She couldn't fix her own problems, let alone all that had been entrusted to her.

"Sonia Ocampo," a deep voice said.

Sonia whipped around and stuffed the *milagros* away. There was a man's figure at the base of the bridge, and he was approaching her quickly. She thought at once of Umberto Masón's cologned hands all over her again, and her heart raced. Had he come back unexpectedly? How far would her scream carry?

"Stay where you are," she ordered.

But the intruder did nothing of the sort. Instead, he stepped out of the shadows. When the moonlight revealed him in its reddish light, Sonia was sure he was a ghost.

His arm was bandaged in a sling. His clothes were torn,

and he smelled strongly of horses. But he was smiling at her with his whole handsome face.

"Pancho?"

He took off his cap as he climbed the slope toward her.

"I did not see you off at the train," he said quietly when he reached her. "It was rude of me; I'm so sorry."

Sonia stared into his face. Nothing made sense.

"But what are you doing here? You didn't come all this way to tell me that."

He scarcely knew what to say, though he had practiced for hours. There was no time to tell her about Conchita Fo or Iguana or Mongo or the train or how her name was a blanket for him each and every night.

"There is no time for explanations." He put his muddy jacket over her shoulders. "You must come with me tonight. Right now."

"What? That's impossible."

"We have to find Rafael," he blurted out.

There were a million questions that might have been asked, but for Sonia all of them were answered in the expression in Pancho's eyes and the way he held out his good hand. She looked at the lights burning in La Casita and imagined the landslide of abuse that would ensue when it was discovered that she'd run away — this time with a boy she loved. Her life as an apprentice in the capital would be over for good.

"Trust me," he said.

Somewhere in the distance, the dogs began their frantic barking. The garage doors swung open, and Oscar pulled the car slowly onto the path. Señora Masón was leaving at last for her party.

"This way." Sonia guided Pancho into the shadows, where they huddled close together, listening to each other breathe.

When the gates finally closed and the taillights faded, she laced her fingers with his and let him lead her to a space he had hacked in the hedges.

"Where did you get that knife?" she said, eyeing the fearsome blade he slipped back inside his sling.

But Pancho only raised her hand to his lips and kissed it. A shiver ran along her arms.

Soon they were dashing through the night like thieves.

Chapter 28

The Arrangements in Colonia Vásquez

THE CAPITAL WAS unrecognizable in its night cloak. They rode the last trolley through streets that were noisy with revelers. Musicians serenaded passersby at every corner, and young couples kissed with such abandon that Sonia blushed. In the distance, the presidential palace glowed proudly, the golden domes reflecting in Pancho's eyes.

One by one, passengers disembarked until only they were left riding the increasingly dark turns.

"Are you sure we shouldn't get off?" she whispered. Her map was back in her bedroom. Nothing here looked familiar.

Pancho shook his head and slid closer. "Not yet."

At last, the conductor reached the end of the line and turned to them.

"Have you two missed your stop?" He frowned and looked around dubiously. "There won't be another trolley out of this place until the morning, you know."

"No, *señor*, we haven't missed it. Thank you for the ride."

Sonia had to fight the urge to run after the trolley as it reversed itself and chugged out of view. The lampposts here were rusted and dim, and store windows were boarded shut.

"We have to hurry," Pancho said.

Sonia read the broken sign as they walked on.

COLONIA VÁSQUEZ.

Long ago Colonia Vásquez had been a neighborhood of well-built Spanish houses carved into the mountainside. Now the homes clung to the cliffs like dying monsters, nothing more than crumbling archways strung with laundry lines. Barefoot children ran yelling in the alleys as bored-looking women looked out over the disaster.

"An item for you, *guapa*?" a man called from his pawnshop doorway. "I have combs for silky hair like yours!"

Sonia glanced in his window. It was filled with unmatched jewelry, hand mirrors, vases, pots—all stolen from the finest houses, she was sure.

Her mind was a blur as she followed Pancho down one

street after another. What business would they have here? And how did this involve Rafael? Pancho had refused to tell her anything so far.

She had just resolved to demand answers when someone stepped into their path. Sonia started to scream, but the man pressed his massive hand against her mouth and shoved her against a building. She bit at his fingers until she tasted blood. Pancho drew his knife.

"Careful with that thing!" The attacker bared his fangs. "You could have quartered me!"

"Oh, it's you, Mongo," Pancho said. "You have a nasty habit of surprising me. Better warning, please."

Mongo looked around and scowled.

"So that the *guardia* can catch sight of me in these parts? Don't be stupid! Policemen have long memories. And then what good would I do her brother from a jail cell?"

Sonia, still pressed against the wall, looked in shock from his face to Pancho's. She pried his fingers from her mouth.

"Who are you and what do you know about my brother?" Her eyes trailed along the tips of the tattooed flames on his neck.

He pulled up his collar.

"Mongo. Follow me," he said, and dashed off.

❖ ❖ ❖

At last they turned down an alley. Mongo stopped at a door and pounded three times.

"Come on, you son of a monkey! Open up, or I'll slice off your other ear," he growled.

"What is this place?" Sonia whispered to Pancho, who was looking less confident by the minute.

He slipped his arm around her waist and drew her closer. "I don't know exactly, but I think we have to trust him. Mongo has been a true friend so far."

Sonia gave him a doubtful look. "He could still hurt us." A shout and breaking glass sounded somewhere nearby. "He could sell us for money. Even that happens here. This is nothing like Tres Montes."

Pancho swallowed hard. "We can turn back, if you wish, but . . ."

Just then they heard footsteps. A tiny man with nervous eyes threw open the door. Mongo pushed past him without a word and climbed up the sagging stairs. He turned and looked impatiently at the two still waiting below.

"Do you want Rafael alive or not?"

"Let's go." Sonia rushed up the steps after him.

The man was named only Hector, and he was missing an ear. The hole in the side of his head was all Sonia could stare at as their host paced.

"So you're back in town," Hector said, smiling at Mongo. "It's been a while since you've been in these parts, my friend. Lots of good old times, eh?"

Mongo sat down and put his feet up on the table.

"Some close shaves, you mean." He picked his nails with the tip of a knife. "But let's get to the point: I need to contact Iguana. He has something I want back. Well . . ." He pointed at Sonia with the blade. "Something of *hers*, actually."

"Iguana?" Sonia repeated, staring for a long moment at Pancho. "You found out what that means?"

Pancho gazed at the ceiling for a moment, as if searching for the right words among the cobwebs and cracked plaster.

"Iguana is the man who has Rafael," he said finally.

"*¿Un pollero?*" she asked.

Hector slapped Mongo on the back.

"Iguana a transporter! Ha-ha! That is a fine joke, is it not?"

Mongo's dark expression withered his joy on the spot.

"*¿Entonces qué?*" Sonia insisted. "If Iguana is not a driver, what is he, then? And what has he done with Rafael?"

Pancho looked at Mongo helplessly.

"He's not a driver. He waits in the valley and detains

travelers coming through on the way north," Mongo said. "Detours them, so to speak, by prior secret arrangement with Conchita Fo and others. When they pay him more money, he lets them go. Conchita gets her share of the extra sum."

Sonia's eyes widened.

"You're telling me Rafael has been *kidnapped*?" Her words hung in the air like dark ash before settling on Pancho's shoulders.

"Don't look so surprised," Hector said. "You can steal a boy as easily as you can steal a woman's purse. Who's out there in La Fuente to help? Ghosts?" He started to laugh again but thought better of it when Mongo shot him another glare.

"I don't believe it." Sonia crossed her arms. "Rafael wouldn't have arranged something so risky. He told me he knew what to do. He's smart; he'd never make such a deal."

Pancho cleared his throat and shifted in his chair. "I took him to Conchita myself, Sonia. He asked me to do it. I saw him pay her with my own eyes. How would he know he was being fooled?" He reached for her hand. "I'm sorry I couldn't tell you. But I didn't know he was walking right into danger."

A long silence followed as the facts fell into place in her mind.

"And what if the traveler has no more money to pay?" Sonia asked slowly, looking from Pancho to Mongo. "He would have spent all he had just to get a driver."

Mongo's face darkened as he leaned toward her. "He hasn't called to ask you for money? You haven't heard from him at all?"

"Bad news," Hector muttered.

Mongo stabbed the table with his dagger. "Shut up."

Sonia was starting to understand everything now. Rafael would rather have chewed off his own hands than ask their father or anyone else for help. But what happened to boys who couldn't find someone to pay for their escape? Did they end up dead like Luis?

"What do we do now?" Pancho asked. "How do we get him back?"

Mongo shook his head as he carved a number into the table with care.

"We pay, what else? There may still be time." He jammed his blade into the tabletop. "If I remember correctly, this amount will do. Not a penny less, though. He's particular about proper ransoms."

He motioned at Hector, who was listening from the corner.

"What are you waiting for, imbecile? Get him on the phone at once! We don't want him to do anything hasty."

Sonia and Pancho gaped at the figure that Mongo had carved.

"I don't have this!" Sonia blurted out. "It would take me months to earn it!"

"And I don't have any money, either." Pancho turned out his pockets as proof.

Mongo sighed with disappointment.

"Well, you'd better find it, friends. Without a ransom, your brother is a corpse."

"Don't say such things!" Sonia sprang to her feet. "There must be something else we can do! What you ask is impossible!"

Mongo shrugged. "Only if you decide it is."

"Really, Mongo, this is no time for riddles," Pancho snapped. "Tell us plainly what we can do."

"I thought you two would be more clever." He leaned back and then motioned at Sonia's clothes. "I can see from your uniform that you work for a rich house."

"For Casa Masón, yes," Sonia admitted. "So?"

"So, that is very fortunate in a case like this. Katarina Masón is the wealthiest woman in the capital, except for the president's wife, as you know." Mongo smiled in satisfaction. "So you see, the situation is not hopeless. The answer is under your nose."

Sonia shook her head in confusion. "I can't ask her for

money. Señora Masón barely speaks to us. Even her orders come through her housekeeper. She'd never do it, especially not for me."

"No," Mongo agreed. "She won't *give* it to you. The rich never part with their money easily. But there are other ways to get what you need, no?"

Sonia held his gaze until his meaning became clear. "You're telling me to steal money from Katarina Masón?"

"*Stealing.* That's such an ugly way to put it. Redistributing is much better."

"It's no solution at all," Sonia said sharply. "I am not like one of the patrons of Conchita's bar. And even if I *were*, I don't know where she keeps her money—only her jewelry."

Mongo grinned like a shark. "Even better. It's a very fine collection, I'm told. The envy of every woman in the capital—and the dream of every crooked jeweler across the continent."

He paused and held up his hands as if they were scales in a balance. The indigo flames etched in his skin reached over his wrists toward his fingers.

"I'm afraid the choice is simple, Sonia Ocampo. Steal the jewels to pay the ransom. Or you keep your sweet honor—and your brother dies. Choose."

Sonia stared at the imaginary scale. Her mind went to

Luis and the dull thud of dirt hitting his coffin. The same could happen to Rafael.

She crossed to the window. Katarina Masón would be at her dinner for hours, enjoying oysters and champagne. The bedroom would be empty, and the jewels sitting safely in the bureau drawer where she'd left them. They were candies in a box, meaningless little trifles that a rich woman could easily replace. Wasn't Rafael's life worth more? She was already a fraud. She'd been called a hussy. Now she was considering stealing from her employer. But what did it matter when her brother's life was at stake?

"I'll do it." She was already imagining the dresser key in her hand.

"No, Sonia—" Pancho began.

"I'll steal the jewels," she said.

CHAPTER 29
Loving Thieves

PANCHO GAVE SONIA a sidelong glance as they hurried through the city. It would be a long walk back to Casa Masón without the trolley, such an intolerable distance to wonder whether she would ever forgive him for having taken Rafael on his errand and not told her. He did his best to ignore her wet cheeks. Even weeping, she was beautiful, but it seemed wrong to say so under the circumstances.

They had agreed to return to Hector's apartment with the jewels at the appointed time. The Iguana had been unreachable by phone, and Mongo—making inquiries among his old cohorts—had decided he would wait for their return and ride all night into the valley to deliver the stolen jewels in person. Then he would return Rafael to them in Tres Montes.

"I'm making no promises, you understand?" he'd said. "Your brother has been missing for a long while, Sonia, and Iguana is not a patient man."

It was already nearing ten o'clock.

"I wish I'd never taken him to Conchita Fo," Pancho said. "I'm sorry."

Sonia wiped the tears off her chin and turned to him.

"Me, too. But if it weren't for you, I would never have known what happened to him—and had the chance to save him. He'd just be another one of those disappeared boys. . . ." She sighed heavily. "You are a true friend, Pancho."

A friend? he wondered, a bit crushed. *Only that?*

He put his hands inside his empty pockets and walked on, lost in his thoughts.

When they reached the edge of the plaza, Sonia sat down on a bench facing the distant statue of the president. Under other circumstances, this would have been a perfect place to visit together. Pancho had spent his life longing to see it. Now it didn't seem to matter much to either of them. Pigeons pecked around their feet expectantly.

"I've been thinking about things," Sonia said. "If I'm caught, there will be trouble. My whole family will be shamed. I don't want that to happen to you, too."

Pancho thought of the mangled bicycle, and Marco's ugly face as he'd tossed him from the train like rubbish.

"You don't have to worry about that," he said. "I'm used to shame."

"Please, Pancho," she insisted. "You've done enough for me already. Go back to Señor Pasqual. He's probably crazy with worry."

Pancho turned out a few crumbs from his pockets for the birds.

"You're not going back alone," he replied. "I'm going with you."

"Pancho Muñoz, you are no criminal. You're a poet."

"And you are—"

Sonia put her hands to his mouth.

"Stop. Don't say it!"

Pancho snapped his mouth shut just in time. He'd been about to say, *You are the girl I love.* He took in the scent of her palm and waited.

"Don't say I'm special—that I'm magic! That's the whole trouble! *Ay*, Pancho! You have no idea of the things that I am—or the things I am not." Another huge tear rolled along her cheek.

Pancho sat quietly, listening to a distant rumble of thunder gathering somewhere on the other side of the mountains. A storm would make their errand even harder.

"I hate secrets," Sonia whispered at last.

"They come with too high a price," he agreed. "They can hurt people we never intend to hurt."

Sonia gave him a long look. She took a deep breath and pulled the bag of *milagros* from her pocket.

"Then maybe it's time to tell them."

Every fiber in Pancho's body twitched as she turned and slipped her hand in his.

"I have a story for *you* this time, Pancho," Sonia began. "It's about a girl who lived a terrible lie. When she was born, people said she had been sent to them by God to carry their burdens and intercede for them. They said she was magic. They loved her for the protection she gave them."

Pancho blinked.

"The trouble is," she continued, "she didn't want to be their protector. It was a burden to carry everyone's woes, and it made her afraid that she would fail them. And one day it happened. She was asked to save a boy, but it was useless. He died in the worst way, and after that it felt to her as if his blood was on her hands. She was too ashamed to tell her friends and neighbors that she couldn't help them, that her voice was no more special in God's ear than their own. She started to hate them for calling on her when they needed something. So she ran away like a coward, rather than telling them that they were wrong about her."

For all the times he'd secretly longed to kiss her, Pancho had never imagined that it would be at this, the very worst moment of his life. But he took her face in his dirty hands and pulled her close until their eyelashes were brushing. He pressed his mouth softly over hers. When he was through, he wiped the tears from each of her cheeks and spoke in her ear.

"But you've forgotten an important part of your story, Sonia," he whispered. "That the girl *was* magic—"

"No—"

"But magic in a different way altogether, and one that she never imagined. For the girl had a light so warm and kind that she could work miracles without even knowing it. She could comfort people just by being in the same room. She could even make a worthless orphan feel like he had something to offer the world."

Sonia looked up at him in surprise. He gave her another long kiss, this time pressing her tight to make sure he wasn't dreaming.

Sonia wrapped her arms around his neck.

"Please tell me how this story ends, Pancho. I'm afraid."

But, of course, he didn't know, and time was running out. The church bells were tolling.

Sonia got to her feet, forgetting the satchel in her lap. Charms scattered to the ground.

"I'll get them," he said.

Sonia stared at the mess as if in another trance.

"What is it?" Pancho asked, noticing her staring.

"Why didn't I think of this before?" Sonia fell to her knees and kissed his hands, his lips. "Hurry and gather them, Pancho! I think I know what to do!"

CHAPTER 30
Miracles for Sale

THEY DASHED BACK through Colonia Vásquez, Pancho looking up worriedly at the sky. The night had taken on an unnatural hue under the red moon. The sky rumbled and flashed. A storm that had been coming from somewhere over the mountains was now upon them.

"Where are we going, Sonia?" Pancho dodged after her as they ran down one decrepit street after another. "Casa Masón is the other way entirely, and we have little time."

"Exactly!" Sonia cried, rounding the next corner. "Follow me!"

The cool drizzle grew heavier until at last the sky gave way. Sonia leaped over puddles, never slowing until she reached an empty corner. The pelting rain was making a second skin of their clothes.

At last she pointed at a dark shop they had passed earlier.

"There it is!"

She pulled Pancho into the brick doorway and banged on the door until the lights clicked on.

"Open up!" she cried.

A few moments later, the shopkeeper appeared from the back room. He was naked to his hairy waist, and it was obvious from his tousled hair that he'd been roused from sleep. He stared at the two soaked cats on his doorstep and motioned them to move on.

"Go beg someplace else!" he shouted through the glass.

Sonia wiped the water from her eyes.

"We're here on business, *señor.*"

"I'm closed. Come back in the morning."

He waved them off again and turned to go, but Sonia rattled the locked doorknob.

"It can't wait. And you stand to make a great deal of money."

The man turned back slowly and opened the door.

The display cases were filled with spoons and clocks, porcelain dolls and engraved pen sets, even two redhead wigs made in Italy. Several silver hairbrushes and matching mirrors lay on a square of velour.

"Well? What have you got?" The shopkeeper looked with irritation at the puddle gathering at Sonia's feet. "It had better be more than filched silverware."

"Oh, it is." Sonia emptied her leather bag of *milagros* as Pancho's eyes grew wide. The metals were luminous, even in the dim light overhead. "What will you give me for these?" she asked.

The shopkeeper ran his fingers through the glittering pile, with a bored look on his face. "They're crude pieces, not worth very much," he said as he turned the tiny treasures under his jeweler's glass. "Superstitious charms — why would I want them?"

"Because they're made of the purest metal — and you know it," Sonia replied. "The metal is clearly exquisite; melted down, it could fill your coffers nicely. How much?"

Sonia peered at the number that the man wrote on a slip of paper. It was just shy of what they needed.

Without blinking an eye, she began to scoop the *milagros* back inside their bag.

"What a shame, *señor*," she said. "It is obvious you don't know what they're really worth. Let's go, Pancho. We have no time to waste here."

In a flash, the man put his hand on hers. "What's the haste? You're so eager to be out in the storm again?"

"Make a better offer, then," Sonia demanded. "It's

mountain metal we're talking about. I'm a miner's girl. You and I both know it's the best in the continent—no matter what fancy city people like to tell themselves about their baubles."

When she glanced his way, Sonia noticed Pancho was beaming.

The shopkeeper scratched his belly, thinking.

"Well?" Sonia asked.

"Let me see what I can do."

He dropped the first piece on his scale.

CHAPTER 31
Dos Mundos

THEY HAD LEFT in the night, just as Mongo had instructed. Unlike the weekend train that ended in Tres Montes, the midweek train ran only as far as the town of Río Negro; they would have to walk the rest of the way.

The journey back through the mountains seemed interminable. All day and night, Sonia stared out into the blackness of La Fuente, searching for signs of travelers among the pallid cows in the hillsides, listening for any moan or shadow that might really be Rafael. When they reached the last stop, they were still more than nine kilometers from home, but Sonia was grateful for the chance to walk in the open air. She might see Rafael, find him herself, somehow.

Of course, she saw no sign of him, only rusted tracks leading home. To distract her, Pancho told her stories until he was hoarse. And he wrapped his arm around her shoulder for comfort. Finally, when they were sure they could not walk another step, Tres Montes appeared before them in the valley.

Sonia took in the view as if she were a traveler from far away. She'd known this village all her life, every path, every shop, every family. Señor Pasqual's taxi boys were milling around for fares. Shopkeepers were unlatching their doors and shooing the stray dogs that warmed themselves on their porches. Tres Montes was unchanged, and yet nothing felt the same as she looked at her home.

She glanced at Pancho from the corner of her eye for strength. His gaze was in the pines rising up along the hillside as she took his hand.

"What are you thinking?" she asked.

"That it's good to be home," he said.

It wasn't until Pancho and Sonia were almost upon them that the taxi boys recognized their old friend trudging along the tracks. In a flash, a fleet of bicycles came racing in their direction, shouts and questions firing as they approached.

"Is it really you, Pancho?"

"Wait until Señor Pasqual sees you!"

"What's wrong with your arm?"

"You smell half dead!"

Armando's voice was loudest of all as he hugged his old friend.

"I ought to yank your ears for all the worry you've caused!"

Sonia was cheered by Pancho's clamoring companions. He put his good arm around her to protect her from the jostling and whistled to silence the racket. The boys fell into a stunned hush.

"Yes, it's me, but I can't tell you anything now. We're in a hurry to get to the Ocampos'."

"Get in, both of you," Armando said quickly. "I can get you there the fastest."

Sonia walked through her empty house. It looked tiny and dirty, and it stank of copal incense, instead of jasmine. The floors were bare wood planks. No one was inside.

"Out here," Pancho called from the backyard.

When she reached the garden, she stood blinking in disbelief. Felix and Blanca Ocampo sat side by side on a bench, every vine and shoot in their plot withered to dust. Their prized vegetables were gone. Felix had shrunk to a sack of bones, and Blanca was sitting idle for the first time Sonia could remember, as if waiting for some apparition to materialize in a spot up ahead.

Tía Neli was the first to see them. She dropped the blanket she was tucking around Felix and rushed across the yard.

"Thank God you're here," she whispered, hugging them both.

Felix swiveled his bony neck in their direction. He seemed lost, and he looked at Sonia warily.

"It's me, Papi," she said in his ear when she reached him. "I'm home."

Felix clutched her old shawl in his lap, and Sonia felt suddenly awkward in her soiled maid's uniform.

"He's still missing," Felix said.

Sonia pressed her lips to his hands; the skin was papery and gray.

"I know. We've sent someone to find him," she said.

Pancho came to stand by her side.

Near evening, Sonia paused behind her screen door. Mongo did not knock but stood in the path, casting a long shadow on the floor she was sweeping. Despite his low hat, she recognized him by his tattoos at once, but she couldn't bring herself to say a word. He jerked his thumb toward the road.

"I've found him."

Sonia's scream pierced the air. Rafael lay like a sack across Mongo's horse. Pancho raced out at once. Felix wobbled from the house in a haze as Blanca ran past him, reaching out in desperation. From every direction, neighbors rushed up the incline in alarm. Mongo's horse neighed and reared.

"Stay back, *señores!*" Pancho shouted.

But it was no use. They pressed forward to look with horror at Rafael.

Sonia rushed to tear at the ropes that bound him. He'd been savaged. His face was bloated and caked with pebbles. Blood soaked his shirtsleeves; two fingers had been hacked off completely. She bit on her lips to keep from vomiting.

Mongo unsheathed his knife and sliced through the ropes to free him faster.

"Dumped," he whispered to her. "I found him like this on the road. "He's barely alive."

"Help me get him inside!" Sonia scooped her arms beneath Rafael's sagging legs. His back arched awkwardly as she and Pancho tugged. She shouted frantically at her neighbors. "Help us!"

But when no one moved, Sonia realized that fear had risen like a poison miasma over the people who had once adored her. Skinned raw of their fantasies about her powers of protection, they stared at her now in terror and doubt. If God could punish her in this way, what might he do next?

Sonia looked from one frightened face to another, realizing her family was abandoned. Fury boiled in her veins as she read their accusing thoughts.

"Look away from us with those eyes, all of you! There is no sin here!"

She turned to Tía Neli instead. "Go at once to Ernesto Fermín. Tell him to send back a doctor from Río Negro or anyplace else he can."

"A doctor?" Tía Neli asked. "No doctor will trouble himself to come here."

"Take that." She pointed at the sack of ransom money still tied to Mongo's belt. "And take Mongo and Pancho with you. There's plenty of cash in that sack to make it worth Capitán Fermín's trouble. Believe me, Tía, he owes us well for ignoring what was under his nose about his girlfriend, Conchita Fo!" She turned to Pancho and lowered her voice. "If he refuses, tell him you'll go straight to his wife."

At last she saw her father staring from the doorway. He dropped her shawl to the ground and walked toward her. He'd been strong once, with eyes that stayed dry no matter how many boys he saw killed in the mines. Live wires in puddles. Cave-ins. Coughs that rattled inside them all the way to Death's door. He'd resigned himself every time.

But now Sonia could see that nothing was more fragile than a man stripped of his illusions. He looked ancient. Inside his eyes was a sadness she had never seen before. With the last of his strength, he picked up his only son and brought him inside.

They worked with a single purpose in the bedroom.

Sonia ripped open Rafael's shirt, biting her tongue when she saw the damage. The skin around his ribs was welted in purple and green, and it was hot to the touch. She bandaged his hand tight with a rag to stop the river of blood from his missing fingers. Blanca washed the dirt and dried blood from his nostrils and lips. His teeth were broken from the gums. Each time a gurgle bubbled in his throat, Sonia crossed herself in case he was taking his last breath.

They worked under Felix's empty stare until Rafael was swaddled in sheets. Sonia stood back, panting and perspired. She wanted to keep working, to find some way to make Rafael better, but there was nothing left to do now but wait for help to arrive. The only sound in the room was Rafael's labored breathing.

Finally, Felix spoke up. "God has found the just punishment."

Sonia set her jaw and turned to him slowly. "And what was Rafael's sin, Papi, that he should be punished like this?" she spat. "Not wanting to work in the mines? Hoping for something better in his life? Is this the God you believe in?"

Blanca held up her hand. "Quiet, both of you," she said. "This is no time for angry words."

But Felix shook his head. "God does the right thing by crooked ways, Blanca. You know that as well as I do."

Sonia froze. Her fingernails were brown with her brother's blood; her feet were tangled in his shredded clothes that stank of urine and infection. She gathered the mess at her feet and headed outside before her father could see her cry.

"Wait—" Felix called.

But Sonia would not listen.

The yard was empty. Though she had always loathed their ceremonies, Sonia found that she longed for the companionship and support that her neighbors might have offered. There were no songs for the ill or incense, and no women guarding the gate to keep out spirits who might want to snatch him away. She hated the sting of loneliness.

Fear had poisoned everyone she knew. It was killing the people of Tres Montes in one way or another. It had left them with no prayers of their own for God, no faith in themselves to face the unknown. No way to be consoled or offer respite to anyone else.

The cooking fire, where Blanca had boiled water, was still smoldering when Sonia reached it. She dropped Rafael's soiled clothes into it and watched the flames lick high into the air.

Then her eyes fell on her shawl. It lay exactly where Felix had dropped it near the doorway. Sonia began to reach for it, deciding on the spot to turn the wretched thing to ash, too. But when she stooped, something surprised her inside the nearby bushes. A pair of eyes was watching her from between the branches.

She took a step closer to get a better look.

It was Luz, a girl who'd once burned with fever, but had recovered as Sonia prayed for her.

"I'm hiding like a panther," the girl said. She made her hands into claws and growled.

"Oh. You're a very good panther, then."

Luz edged out, grinning wide as she wrapped herself around Sonia's legs. The warmth of her little body was instantly calming. Sonia thought of the copper charm that stood for Luz on her shawl. Time had already given it the desirable tinge of verdigris. Would time be as generous to the real girl in a place like Tres Montes? What would it offer?

Sonia ruffled her hair.

"Go on, now, before your mother finds you," she said. "We shouldn't both be in trouble."

In a flash, Luz's bare feet were slapping against the packed dirt.

By nightfall, when her parents at last dozed in their chairs, Sonia stared out into the dusk, trying to not to think about sleep. She was too afraid to close her eyes and lose Rafael, who looked smaller and more fragile with each passing hour.

Instead, she listened to the night sounds. For all its grandeur, there was no music like this in the capital. Nor did the breeze circle the treetops in the same way. She took in deep breaths, until a rustle in the room made her turn.

Abuela had slipped into a corner, looking at Rafael with pity.

"Don't take him yet," Sonia said. "Please."

Abuela sighed and made Sonia's eyelids heavy. Good memories blew through the room. Learning to swim in the river, roasting chicken legs on the fire, searching for lizards after rains, running the cliffs, even the Saturday-morning arguments at market. The images took shape before Sonia's sleepy eyes and floated away to Felix and Blanca, until soon their slack lips curled into smiles.

Sonia reached for Rafael's hand. It was ice. She lay down beside him and whispered in his ear.

She murmured stories about the capital, pretending she could still see the mischief in his eyes. She promised him the largest truck that money could buy and apologized for every moment she had ever secretly envied him. His breaths grew shallow, and a strong odor of sulfur filtered through his bandages. She tried not to notice the red streaks of infection running the length of his wounded arm.

It was nearly dawn by the time Tía Neli, Pancho, and Mongo arrived with the doctor, a tired-looking man who'd been battling spotted fever in the countryside. Mongo's horse had a glazed look; its ears were limp from the long trip. The group rushed up the path and stopped when they saw her.

Sonia was in the yard alone, staring at the embers that still glowed in the fire pit. Bits of Rafael's charred belt were smoldering. For a moment, no one spoke.

"We've brought the doctor," Pancho said.

She turned to him slowly.

"Abuela came," she replied.

Tía Neli covered her mouth and raced inside with the others, the screen door banging behind her. Sonia didn't follow. She stared at the last of the fire once again.

Rafael was gone.

CHAPTER 32
Farewells

THERE WERE NO songs or processions. No long wails of neighbors coiling into the sky, only Señora Clara tucking mint leaves gently inside Rafael's cheeks as she prepared him in his father's best coat.

The next day he was buried quietly in a spot not far from Abuela and Luis, where Sonia said he could look out over the train whenever he liked.

"He didn't deserve that fate," Pancho whispered to Mongo, who had dug a grave through the moss and rocky earth while Pancho watched hopelessly, his arm still useless from his untimely exit from the train. That pain, however, was nothing compared to watching Sonia's private despair.

The barkeep wiped the sweat from his head and loaded the last shovel onto his horse. He shook his head and clapped his young friend on the back.

"Don't waste your time on such thoughts, Pancho. Fate meets the lucky and unlucky every day. There's no use thinking it's any other way."

They finished packing in silence.

"Where will you go now?" Pancho asked him when he mounted at last. Conchita Fo had disappeared for parts unknown, according to Armando. La Jalada was deserted.

Mongo shrugged. "Who knows? Wherever the wind takes me, I suppose. But don't worry. I'll send word when I get settled; then you can write me more of your stories." He hit his forehead with his hand. "Oh. I almost forgot."

He fished in his pocket and drew out the remaining money that the *milagros* had fetched in the capital. "Give it back to her. Her people will need it from the looks of things."

Pancho pocketed the money for safekeeping and watched his friend disappear into the trees. Then he joined Sonia near the fig tree. She and Tía Neli sat away from her parents. The space between them reminded Pancho of a chasm between mountains, but this one seemed to have no bridge. No one was speaking.

He tossed a small sack of wildflower seeds on the ground.

"For planting," he said. Next year, when the ground

237

was flat and hard again, he thought it would be a comfort to see their color, the bees dawdling heavily in the blooms.

Sonia stared, and Pancho instantly knew what she was thinking. Next year she would still be here without Rafael. By then she might start to forget the sound of her brother's voice.

"*Gracias*, Pancho," Tía Neli said. "We'll plant them before we go."

But the hours went by, and they walked home in gloom. No one had mustered the will to plant the seeds.

The next day, when Pancho arrived at the grave to spread the seeds himself, he found that Sonia was already there. She was sitting at the very edge of the outcrop, watching the hawks in the canyon. Her shawl lay beside her. She'd removed every charm from the fabric and piled them at the foot of the fig tree. Clearly, it had taken her hours of work. Her fingertips were bloody from the pricks. Her clothes were damp with dew.

He sat down and put his arm around her shoulders. From here they could see the river and the tracks, even the roof of Irina Gomez's dilapidated schoolhouse and the shade tree where they'd shared so many stories.

"One day it will feel a little better," he said, thinking of long ago when he had become an orphan.

Sonia picked up her shawl and rubbed her fingers along the fabric.

"I need to trouble you with another favor," she said.

"Of course, anything. What is it?"

"Bring my parents here. Will you do that for me?"

"What should I tell them?"

Sonia sighed. She'd been asking herself that same question all night.

"Just bring them."

Sonia was waiting when Pancho returned with her parents and Tía Neli. She was standing at the edge of the outcrop with her bare shawl on her shoulders. Tía Neli, still in her apron, gave her a worried look. Felix and Blanca stood watching her in awkward silence.

"Is your plan to finish us off by scaring us to death, Sonia?" Tía Neli asked. "Come away from there."

But Sonia did not move.

"There are other more important things that need to be finished off," Sonia said. "Things that should have been stopped long ago."

She held out the remains of Abuela's gauzy shawl, light

as a whisper without any of the charms. When she opened her hands, it was snatched by the wind and carried far up into the drafts of the canyon. Blanca and Felix watched, speechless, as it sailed out of view.

Finally, Sonia came to their side.

"I would have saved him if I could have," she said. "But I'm no more a savior than anyone else, Papi. I wish I could be what you hope for. All I am is Sonia."

Felix cast down his eyes.

"God does the right thing by crooked paths," he repeated. "This *is* the just punishment for sin."

He caught her by the elbow as she started to walk off. His grip was still firm. "The sins here have been mine all along, *hija*."

Sonia looked into his face. Felix's lips were trembling.

"Look at what I've done with my bull-headedness. I asked a young man to give up hope for a future. I made a girl carry the burdens I was too weak to carry myself. For all I've done, there is no forgiveness. I'm cursed. All I can do is beg you to have pity on me, Sonia."

Sonia buried her face in his shoulder. Soon Felix drew his wife and daughter closer.

"We can make things right again. Your brother wanted a future, one that he chose for himself. He knew he deserved one, and so do you. I don't want him to have died for nothing."

Blanca took his hand and kissed it. She ran her hands along Sonia's hair.

"I knew she wouldn't come back the same," Blanca said. "But I never imagined she would come back so strong."

"If you will permit me . . ."

Sonia lifted her head to find that Pancho had joined them. He offered his elbow and walked her parents to the fig tree, where Tía Neli was already waiting. A single *milagro* was hanging from a strip of cloth on the lowest branch. It was the charm Rafael had given Sonia. . . . A silver eye for wisdom and clarity.

"Pancho and I think this silly tree has always looked too bare." She surveyed the canopy with misty eyes. "I can't stand the sight of it another minute."

Pancho held out the next charm on a strip of Tía Neli's torn apron. He pressed the copper heart into Sonia's hand and cast a cautious glance at Felix, who was looking on.

"Put this one on next," he whispered.

The Ocampos worked together, their feet firmly on the mountain that had seen them born, but their sights high enough to see new possibilities. As the day wore on, news spread from one yard to the next and one by one, the people of Tres Montes gathered to watch them work. By dusk, the limbs of the fig tree glittered with what had once been the prayers of a whole mountain. The *milagros* moved in the breeze and reflected even the dimmest of evening light. Everyone stared in awe at the power and beauty of their own hopes and fears laid bare.

That night the music of charms in the wind guided them home.

CHAPTER 33
The Girl Who Could Silence the Wind

YEARS LATER, SONIA used the money that hadn't been able to save her brother to build a new school for the village. Sometimes she would stand at the door and listen to the music of the Prayer Tree outside. Each year her students added their own hopes and dreams to the branches for all to see. Sharing them, she told the students, was the first step toward helping their dreams come true. This, she thought, was the best way to honor Rafael.

Indeed, mentioning a hope out loud was how Sonia would realize her own dream, although she didn't know it at the time. How could she have guessed that a chat over shaved ice with a chauffeur would lead to this? But it was true. Oscar never forgot Sonia or her bright, intelligent eyes. A few years later, when he died a content old man, a letter arrived for Sonia from the capital. *Teach,* his note said. Inside was the money for her studies. Somehow, he managed to return every penny she had earned during her time in the capital—and then some.

As for Pancho, in time he earned fame for his poems and mountain tales, telling them with the same joy, whether to kindhearted thieves or to men of honor. As Sonia had predicted, he'd become Francisco Muñoz, a favorite of the president and his wife, both of whom tirelessly requested the tale of the Girl Who Could Silence the Wind.

"It's superstition and nonsense," the dignitaries told their friends with embarrassed chuckles.

But Sonia and Pancho knew better. Privately, when they held hands and shared stories under their Prayer Tree, they confessed they had always had a soft spot for old mountain stories like his, for tales of humble people and the courage it took to live their days. For true stories of magic and love.

Meg Medina is the author of the young adult novels *Yaqui Delgado Wants to Kick Your Ass*, winner of the Pura Belpré Author Award, and *Burn Baby Burn* as well as the picture books *Tía Isa Wants a Car*, illustrated by Claudio Muñoz, and *Mango, Abuela, and Me*, for which she received a Pura Belpré Author Honor and illustrator Angela Dominguez received a Pura Belpré Illustrator Honor. Of *The Girl Who Could Silence the Wind*, she says, "I wrote Sonia's story in the tradition of old Latino tales—romantic and magical. But I didn't want a telenovela. I wanted a novel that spoke to what's happening all around us even today. The question I kept asking myself as I developed the story was: What is it that all young people deserve, regardless of where they're born or their station in life? To me the answer is love, respect, and a chance at a future full of possibility. That's the core. These are the things for which a person will risk everything." The daughter of Cuban immigrants, Meg Medina grew up in Queens, New York, and now lives in Richmond, Virginia.